"She's yo

His mouth snapped shut, his face paled. "Why would you concoct such an outrageous story?"

"It's not a story—it's t
have known telling h
She stood up. "I thou
right to know. But I'd
identity of her father
her."

Jackson pushed away from his desk as she reached for the handle of the door. "Wait." He slapped his hand against the frame. "You can't drop a bombshell like that and just walk out."

He stood so close that he breathed in her hauntingly familiar scent. Memories of that long-ago weekend teased his mind, and something stirred low in his belly. Even now, when she was making accusations that could turn his life upside down, he couldn't ignore the heat thrumming in his veins.

"We're done here," she said.

He moved closer. "We're not even close to being done."

Dear Reader,

I've always enjoyed reading "secret baby" stories, but as a writer, it's sometimes difficult to justify a woman's decision to keep her child from the father.

For Kelly Cooper, the situation is further complicated by the fact that the father is her best friend's brother. And when she finally comes home to Pinehurst with her daughter, she knows the truth can't remain a secret any longer.

One marriage and one divorce cured Jackson Garrett of any hopes that he would ever have a family of his own—until he learns that he is the father of Kelly's twelve-year-old daughter.

Kelly and Jackson both have scars from the past, but if they can somehow manage to get over their hurt and anger, they just might find their way to being a family.

This "second chance" is another favorite theme of mine. Everyone makes mistakes and sometimes wishes for a "do over." Unfortunately, the real world doesn't have time machines that enable us to go back and undo what has been done. But if we're lucky, we might get a second chance to make things right.

This story is about Kelly and Jackson's second chance—I hope you enjoy it.

Happy Reading,

Brenda Harlen

His Long-Lost Family

Brenda Harlen

HARLEQUIN® SPECIAL EDITION®

Recycling programs
for this product may
not exist in your area.

ISBN-13: 978-0-373-65760-5

HIS LONG-LOST FAMILY

Copyright © 2013 by Brenda Harlen

Printed in U.S.A.

BRENDA HARLEN

is a former family law attorney turned work-at-home mom and national bestselling author who has written more than twenty books for Harlequin. Her work has been validated by industry awards (including an RWA Golden Heart Award and the *RT Book Reviews* Reviewers' Choice Award) and by the fact that her kids think it's cool that she's "a real author."

Brenda lives in southern Ontario with her husband and two sons. When she isn't at the computer working on her next book, she can probably be found at the arena watching a hockey game. Keep up-to-date with Brenda on Facebook or send her an email at brendaharlen@yahoo.com.

This second book in my series about brothers is dedicated to my brother, Jim, who was part of my inspiration for Jackson Garrett—and who will no doubt experience much of the same angst as this story's hero when his beautiful daughters get to be Ava's age...

With special thanks to Emily Baker for proofreading Ava's scenes to ensure that I wasn't completely out of touch with the current teen generation. Someday you will find a romantic hero worthy of you—in the meantime, enjoy the journey, YOLO

Prologue

Kelly Cooper glanced at her watch as she slipped her feet into a pair of navy blue pumps and bit back an exasperated sigh. Every day, it was the same. No matter what time she woke her daughter, it seemed they were always running behind schedule.

"Come on, Ava. We're going to be late."

The twelve-year-old raced down the hall, her backpack in one hand and a piece of paper in the other.

"Sorry, Mom. I forgot that I need you to sign something."

Kelly dug into her bag for a pen. Her daughter was famous for holding on to trip permission and lunch order forms until the morning that they were due, usually when they were already late getting out the door.

Ava flattened the page out on the table by the door so that Kelly could scrawl her signature on the dotted line. But something about the way her daughter's hand was splayed over the top of the page triggered Kelly's maternal radar. She tugged the page out of Ava's grasp, caught the headline at the top—CONSENT FOR BODY PIERCING OF A MINOR.

When she was sure that she could speak calmly, she turned to her daughter and said, "Nice try, Ava."

"Come on, Mom. *Please*."

"No." She tore the paper in half, then in quarters, and opened the door. "Let's go."

Ava's deep green eyes, the mirror image of her father's, filled with tears. "It's just my belly button."

"It's not *just* anything," Kelly argued. "Which I told you last week when you came home raving about Rachel's sister's hips being pierced. I am *not* letting you permanently disfigure any part of your body with holes or ink."

"Why not?"

"Because you're twelve years old." She locked the door and headed down the hall to the elevator.

"I'm almost thirteen," Ava said.

Actually, she'd only celebrated her twelfth birthday a few months earlier, but that wasn't the issue. "Still nowhere close to eighteen," she pointed out. "If you want a belly button ring when you're eighteen, I won't be able to say no. But until then, that is the answer."

"You're *so* mean."

"You've mentioned that once or twice before," she acknowledged as they exited on the ground floor.

"Miranda and Corinne have belly button rings, and Rachel's getting hers pierced on her birthday." Ava climbed into the passenger side and latched her belt. "Because her mother's cool, and because she believes it's a way for Rachel to express her individuality."

"How can it be an expression of her individuality if she's having it done to be like everyone else?" Kelly countered.

Ava huffed out a breath. "Why do you always have to treat me like a baby?"

"Because you are my baby," she reminded her.

Her daughter was silent for a long minute, but Kelly knew better than to think that she'd given up. It wasn't in Ava's nature to back down on anything. As she proved when she said, "I bet if I had a dad, he'd let me get my belly button pierced."

It was a familiar argument. Whenever Kelly didn't give

her daughter what she wanted, Ava played the no-father card. And while Kelly didn't let the arguments sway her, she couldn't deny the guilt that inevitably swamped her. Because Ava *did* have a father, but she'd never met the man who had contributed to her DNA—and that man had no idea that he had a child.

She tried not to think about him, but she'd never forgotten him. Not since the night of her sixteenth birthday, when he'd kissed her. In that first moment that his lips touched hers, he'd also taken hold of her heart. It was several years later before their relationship progressed beyond that single kiss, before the one weekend they spent together changed her whole life.

He was the only man she'd ever really loved, and when he'd chosen to be with someone else, Kelly had taken her shattered heart and her unborn child and moved as far away as possible. But it turned out that halfway across the country still wasn't far enough to outrun the memories, guilt and regrets.

"This isn't negotiable," she said firmly.

Ava fell silent again, pouting.

On her way to her daughter's school, Kelly tried to remember what she'd been like as a twelve-year-old girl. She'd been shy and withdrawn through most of her childhood, cautiously trying to find her way in the world. Thankfully, she'd had Lukas Garrett to guide her. Maybe it was because her best friend was a boy, but she'd never thought too much about clothes or makeup. She'd never worried about keeping up with fashion trends or trying to attract boyfriends; she'd never dyed her hair or worn black nail polish. And she certainly hadn't been thinking about body piercings or tattoos.

Of course, she'd grown up in a different time, and Pinehurst, New York, was definitely another world. Though fifteen years had passed since she'd first gone away to college and the population of the town had increased exponentially, she knew that not much else had changed. Pinehurst still was, and probably always would be, a small town at heart. It was a place where neighbors talked to one another on the street, where the residents baked cookies to welcome newcomers, and where traditional values continued to be revered. Recently Kelly had found herself thinking that it would be nice to raise her daughter in a town like that.

As she pulled up in front of the school to drop Ava off, her thoughts drifted back to the email Lukas had sent to her the previous day, and she cursed him for tempting her with the link to a job posting at Richmond Pharmaceuticals. Because she *was* tempted and she didn't want to be; because going back to Pinehurst would inevitably mean revealing the secret she'd kept throughout her daughter's entire life.

If she stayed in Seattle, on the other hand, everything would remain status quo. Unfortunately, the status quo was no longer as satisfying as it used to be. And while a cross-country move wouldn't make Ava happy in the short term, Kelly believed it would be the best thing for her—maybe even for both of them—in the long term.

A new start in a new town, a new school, new friends… and maybe even a chance to finally meet her father.

Chapter One

Four months later—

"Sorry I'm late." Jack Garrett slid into the vacant seat across from Gord Adamson, a former law school class-mate and occasional courtroom adversary, at The Winking Judge, a small pub across the street from the courthouse.

"I was surprised to get your call," Gord admitted. "I thought you'd given up criminal law."

"So did I," he agreed. "But every once in a while, there's a client I can't turn away."

"Because you believe in his innocence?"

"Because I believe that he deserves a break."

The waitress came over, momentarily disrupting their conversation. Gord ordered a scotch, neat, and Jack asked for a bottle of the locally brewed Millhouse beer.

"I reviewed the file, Jack. And I'm sorry, but I don't see probation for Travis Hatcher."

"Come on, Gord. He's just a kid."

"A kid who took a baseball bat to a Mercedes that is worth more than twice my annual salary," his colleague pointed out.

"It was his father's car," Jack told him, though even he wasn't sure if that was a mitigating or an aggravating factor.

"With incidental damage to two other vehicles."

"Restitution has already been made to the owners."

Gord sighed. "What's your connection to this kid?"

"I handled his parents' divorce a few years back," Jack admitted.

"Rough one?"

"I don't seem to get any other kind, but this one was particularly difficult. A ten-year marriage that fell apart because the husband couldn't keep his pants zipped and the wife couldn't keep looking the other way. They fought over each piece of artwork and every stick of furniture, but mostly over who was going to get stuck with their ten-year-old son."

Gord, a father with two sons of his own, winced. "Damn, Jack. You're yanking on my heartstrings here."

"He isn't a bad kid," Jack insisted. "He just got caught in a bad situation."

"Give me some background," the prosecutor suggested.

"A few months back, Travis was invited to a weekend camp to try out for the national amateur all-star tournament. There wasn't anyone at the camp who doubted he would make the team. But instead of being offered a roster spot, he was sent home."

"I can understand that he would be disappointed and upset," Gord acknowledged. "But that doesn't justify his actions."

"That's not the end of the story," Jack told him. "About two weeks before the tournament, the number-one center fielder breaks his collarbone. There's no way he can play, so Travis calls the national team coach, asks him to give him another chance to prove that he can fill the vacancy. And the coach bluntly tells him, 'You're good enough, but you're never going to play on any team that I'm coaching. If you want to know why—ask your father.'"

"The kid's dad screwed the coach's wife," Gord guessed.

Jack nodded. "Which he finally admitted when Travis confronted him after baseball practice."

"Jesus." His friend lifted his glass, swallowed a mouthful of scotch.

"There was no premeditation—he had the bat in his hand, and he simply reacted," he explained. "Under the circumstances, can you blame him?"

"Actions have consequences, and he has to be responsible for those consequences."

"Absolutely. But the consequences should be commensurate with the action. He had *a moment* where he acted impulsively and recklessly, but a criminal record will stick with him *for life*."

"You stay up late last night working on that spin?"

"The truth doesn't need spin."

Gord considered that for a moment. "Is he remorseful?"

"Very." Jack passed a handwritten note across the table.

His colleague skimmed the page; he scrubbed a hand over his jaw. "Damn you, Jack."

"You're repeating yourself, Gord." He passed over several more pages. "Character references from his teachers, guidance counselor, principal, high school baseball coach, his boss at the grocery store where he works part-time, and supervisor of the homework club where he volunteers twice a week."

Gord sighed. "You really think you can get probation?"

"With a joint-sentencing recommendation, I do," Jack said.

"I'll go joint if anger management is one of the terms of probation, but the final decision is still up to the judge."

"Of course," he agreed.

Gord took another sip of his drink. "You still dating Angela from the registry office?"

Jack shook his head. "That was over a long time ago."

"No thoughts about settling down and starting a family at this stage in your life?"

"Hell, no." His failed marriage might be in the past, but it wasn't so distant that he'd forgotten. And how could he when he spent almost every day in meetings and motions with husbands and wives who had once promised to love, honor, and cherish their spouses and were now hating, dishonoring, and spurning them?

His friend chuckled. "Are you sure you don't want a minute to consider your response?"

Jack shook his head. "I was married once," he confided. "When I was young and stupid."

"Was it that girl you were with in Chicago?"

Jack paused with his bottle halfway to his lips. He'd forgotten that Gord had been at the same law conference he'd attended more than a dozen years earlier in Chicago. "No," he said now. "That wasn't her."

"So who was she?" Gord asked curiously. "Because I seem to recall that you had some pretty intense chemistry with her."

He frowned, as if trying to recall the details of those three glorious days that were still indelibly imprinted on his mind, then shook his head. "I don't remember."

His friend snorted. "Yeah, and I took a job in the district attorney's office for the extravagant salary."

"Why did you leave private practice?" Jack asked, because it seemed like an opportune moment to shift the topic of conversation.

"Because when Sheila and I got married, she understood that I wanted to get my practice off the ground before I took any time off for a vacation. On our third anniversary, she reminded me that we still hadn't had a honeymoon."

"And yet, you're still married," he mused.

"Because I was smart enough to realize that I needed to balance my personal life and my professional life. Five years and two kids later, it was the smartest move I ever made—even if it means that my kids will have to go to public school."

"Thankfully not something I have to worry about."

"Never say never," Gord warned.

But Jack wasn't worried. He was thirty-seven years old and happy to be on his own. And while he dated—albeit a lot less frequently than he had in the past—he always said goodbye without any regrets. The sole exception was the one unforgettable weekend he'd spent in Chicago with Kelly Cooper.

Yeah, he had a boatload of regrets where she was concerned. He regretted walking into The Four Brothers pub for a drink—and not walking right back out again when he realized the gorgeous bartender who'd snared his attention was none other than the girl who'd lived next door when they were kids.

He regretted giving in to the irresistible urge to taste the sassy mouth that had tormented him for more years than he wanted to admit; he regretted succumbing to the need to explore every inch of her soft, silky skin with his hands and his lips; he regretted losing himself—over and over again—in her warm, willing body. Mostly he regretted ever letting her go.

"Speaking of family," Gord said, drawing Jack's attention back to the present, "I should get home to Sheila and the boys."

He started to call for the waitress, but Jack shook his head. "You go ahead. I've got the bill."

"Thanks." Gord slid out of the booth, offered his hand. "I'll bring your client's case forward for a plea on Wednesday, when Judge Parrish is sitting."

"I appreciate it," he said, confident in the knowledge that Judge Parrish had never overruled a joint recommendation.

After his colleague was gone, Jack sat alone, nursing a

second beer. He was grateful for Gord's cooperation with Travis's case—and annoyed that just the mention of Chicago had brought memories of Kelly Cooper to the forefront of his mind.

Not that those memories were ever very far away, especially not since his brother had informed him that she was coming home.

He didn't understand why she was the one woman he couldn't forget. They'd spent one unforgettable weekend together, but neither of them had mentioned the possibility of anything more. So when Kelly called a few months later—shortly after Sara had decided she'd been too hasty in ending their engagement—he'd been completely caught off guard. Just the sound of her voice had the memories flooding back and desire stirring. Then Sara had walked into the room and pointed to her watch, and he'd admitted to Kelly that he had an appointment with a wedding planner. After a brief moment of awkward silence, Kelly had offered a quick congratulations and an even quicker goodbye.

Six months later, he'd married Sara. About two years after that, Kelly married some guy out in Seattle. Now they were both divorced, and despite all the years that had passed, he hadn't forgotten about her. For some inexplicable reason, memories of one long ago weekend still stirred his blood more effectively than most of the flesh-and-blood women he'd dated in recent years.

Maybe it was because he still felt guilty about the fact that he'd slept with the girl who had been his brother's best friend since childhood. Yeah, it was the guilt, he assured himself.

Because Jack refused to consider that he might have had feelings for Kelly that ever went any deeper than that.

* * *

The knots in Kelly's stomach tightened as the plane touched down on the runway.

This was it—there was definitely no going back now.

Not that she wanted to go back. Although she'd made the decision to move back to Pinehurst quickly, it hadn't been impulsively. Which made her realize she'd been thinking about it for a lot longer than she'd been ready to acknowledge. Because no matter where else she might have lived, Pinehurst was still home.

She'd had such grand plans when she'd moved to Seattle. A new city, a new job, a new husband. Even when she and Malcolm had gone their separate ways, she hadn't wanted to leave Seattle. Of course, Malcolm's mom—the only grandmother Ava had ever known—had still been a big part of their lives. Kelly knew she wouldn't have made it through those first few years without her former mother-in-law, and when Beverley Scott had passed away, she'd been at a loss. Not only because Bev had willingly stepped in whenever Kelly needed someone to watch her little girl, but because the older woman had been Kelly's best friend in Washington.

Now it was time for a fresh start again. After more than a dozen years on the West Coast, she had no regrets about leaving. But she wasn't entirely sure she wouldn't regret coming home.

The plane pulled up at the gate, and the knots multiplied.

Okay, she was more than a little nervous, but she reminded herself that she was doing this for Ava. This decision, like every other decision she'd made since she'd learned that she was pregnant, had been focused on what was best for her daughter. Even if Ava didn't agree.

And the words she spoke, as they made their way off the plane, confirmed that she didn't. "I can't believe you made me leave Seattle to come here," Ava grumbled.

Kelly hadn't expected that her daughter would be over-joyed by her decision, but she had hoped that she would have accepted it by now. "You know, if you weren't so de-termined to hate it, you might actually like it here," she told her.

"I doubt it."

She didn't argue. The choice had been made and their new life was about to begin, so all she said was "Grab your suitcase."

They'd packed only what they needed for a few days, with the rest of their clothes and household items being shipped.

Ava hauled the bag off of the conveyor belt. "How are we getting to Pinecone?"

"Pine*hurst,*" she corrected automatically. "And Uncle Luke said he would pick us up and take us to our new place."

"When are we getting a car?"

"Before August fifteenth," Kelly assured her, because that was the date she was scheduled to start her new job as an in-house accountant at Richmond Pharmaceuticals.

Ava rolled her eyes. With the purple streaks she'd added to her hair during her last sleepover at Rachel's house and the gloomy expression on her face, she looked too much like a typical sullen teenager—and she was still only twelve. As much as Kelly desperately hoped this move would help turn things around with Ava, she knew that any change would take time.

"I'll probably start looking tomorrow," she said, hoping to appease her daughter. "I just wasn't keen on picking up a rental and then driving to Pinehurst after spending all day on airplanes."

"How far is Pinetree?"

"About an hour from here," she said, not bothering to correct her on the name of the town again. Instead, she grabbed the handle of her own suitcase. "Let's go find Uncle Luke."

Kelly headed out of the baggage claim area, then stopped so abruptly Ava plowed right into the back of her.

"Geez, Mom," her daughter grumbled.

Kelly didn't—*couldn't*—respond.

Because standing at the car rental counter, where Lukas said he would be waiting, was his brother, Jackson, instead.

"Mom?" Ava prompted, sounding genuinely concerned. "What's wrong?"

Kelly had to remind herself to breathe, and she exhaled slowly. "Nothing's wrong," she lied, not wanting to alarm her daughter. "I just lost my train of thought for a moment."

"Well, put brake lights on next time," Ava suggested. Then, after looking around, "I don't see Uncle Luke anywhere."

"Apparently there's been a change of plans," Kelly noted, trying to keep her tone light while she inwardly cursed Lukas Garrett all the way to hell and back.

"Does that mean we're going to rent a car?" Ava asked.

"No, it means you're going to meet Uncle Luke's brother."

A lot sooner than I had planned.

She stood for another minute, still rooted to the spot, and just looked at Jackson. She hadn't seen him in thirteen years, but she'd recognized him immediately. But it was more than the dark brown hair that was always immaculately trimmed, more than the exquisitely shaped mouth that had inspired so many of her teenage fantasies, and more than the green eyes that were as dark and clear as emeralds. It was even more than the fact that he was six feet of solidly built male, with broad shoulders and strong arms that ensured any woman would feel secure and protected in his embrace. It was, more than anything else, the way Kelly felt when she looked at him—all hot and tingly and tongue-tied.

Sternly reminding herself that she wasn't still sixteen years old—or even twenty-one—she took a step toward him.

He glanced up from the book he was reading—a legal journal of some kind—as if he sensed her approach. She'd noticed that the book was in his left hand, and that the third finger was bare. But the fact that he'd been divorced for quite a few years now didn't make him any less off-limits.

As he closed the cover of the journal, his gaze skimmed over her, from the top of her head to her toes in a quick, cursory perusal that nevertheless caused heat to flare low in her belly and spread through her veins. She hadn't counted on this, and that was a definite miscalculation on her part.

But how could she have known that, after so many years, he would still have this effect on her? Because even from a distance, even after so much time, she couldn't deny her body's instinctive response to him. Or the ache in her heart.

She pushed her bangs away from her face and silently reprimanded herself for even noticing that her hair was as flat and tired as the rest of her. She'd dressed comfortably for travel in a pair of faded jeans and an ancient University of Chicago sweatshirt and had put on the barest touch of makeup before heading out to the airport more than ten hours earlier. As a result, she felt not just unprepared but ill-equipped to come face-to-face with Jackson now.

When she'd decided to return to Pinehurst, she'd known it was inevitable that she would see him. But she hadn't planned on seeing him when she was looking like *this*. She knew it shouldn't matter, but when a woman was facing an ex-lover, she wanted to look her best. Unfortunately, she wasn't even close.

Those green eyes lifted to her face again. "Hello, Kelly."

Two simple words, but after so many years of silence, the achingly familiar voice was like a warm caress.

Her heart was pounding inside of her chest, but she inclined her head and responded in a similarly casual tone. "Jackson."

His lips curved, just a little, and she suddenly remembered that no one else, aside from his mother, had ever called him "Jackson." At least not more than once. But he'd never been Jack to Kelly—that name was too common, and Jackson was anything but. She had, occasionally, shortened his name to Jacks, but that seemed too familiar now.

He shifted his attention to her daughter again. "You must be Ava."

The girl nodded, her gaze darting from her mother to Jackson and back again, as if she sensed the strange undercurrents between them.

Kelly held her breath, waiting for any sign of recognition. But there wasn't any. And why would there be? Unless Lukas had shared the occasional photos that she'd sent to him, Jackson had never seen her daughter before. But she'd thought he might see some of the familial resemblance that Kelly saw whenever she looked at her little girl.

"I'm Jack Garrett, Luke's brother." He offered his hand.

Kelly fought an almost irresistible urge to cry as she watched them shake hands. It broke her heart to see the distance between them, but what had she expected? It was her fault that neither of them knew the truth of their connection.

Thirteen years ago, Jackson had been focused on his career above all else. He'd been clear that he had no interest in having a family, at least not any time in the near future. That was one of the reasons why Kelly had honestly believed she'd made the right decision. But she didn't know what was right for any of them now.

She wanted Ava to know her father, but only if Jackson

was prepared to *be* a father. And she was afraid to finally reveal the secret she'd kept for so long because she knew that when she did, it was quite possible he would hate her—either for keeping his child from him for so many years… or for bringing her into his life now.

"You seem surprised to see me," Jackson said, speaking to Kelly again as they made their way toward the exit.

Surprised was barely the tip of her emotional iceberg, so she only said, "I was expecting Lukas."

"He said he'd let you know that I'd be meeting you instead."

"Maybe he tried," she admitted, taking her cell out of her purse. "I turned off my phone when we boarded the plane."

She powered it up now and heard the familiar chime that indicated a text message. But since it was written in Luke's unique form of shorthand and without any punctuation, she had to read it twice before she figured out what it said.

Srry kel ER at clinic cant meet u sending j instead will stop by ur plc if not 2 late

Gee, thanks for the warning, Lukas.

"I'm guessing that's his message," Jackson said, his voice tinged with humor as he popped the trunk of his car to load their suitcases.

Of course he would find this amusing. He wasn't the one who'd been blindsided by the change of plans.

"You guessed right," she agreed lightly, then slid into the soft leather passenger seat of his luxury sedan.

Ava was already in the backseat with her mp3 player plugged in, leaving her mother to make conversation with Jackson. But Kelly didn't know what to say. She'd known that she would see him again—but she hadn't expected that he would be the first person she saw at the airport, and she mentally cursed Lukas again.

Of course, he couldn't know what he'd done. After all, he didn't know that his brother was the only man she'd ever really loved.

Well, this is more than a little awkward, Jack thought, as he pulled out onto the highway heading toward Pinehurst. He'd suspected that it would be, considering that the last time he'd seen Kelly, they'd both been naked. Which was definitely *not* something he should be thinking about right now—not under any circumstances and certainly not with her daughter in the backseat.

He tightened his grip on the steering wheel, but the smooth, warm leather beneath his palms made him itch to feel the much softer, warmer texture of Kelly's skin. Not that he really knew what her skin felt like—it was ridiculous to think that he could recall those kind of details after so much time had passed. So why was he convinced that her skin was softer than silk? Why did he remember that her body had responded not just willingly but eagerly to his touch? And why couldn't he forget that, throughout that one weekend they'd spent together, he'd wished it would never end?

Of course it had ended, and they'd gone their separate ways. Since then, they'd both married and divorced other people. The main difference being that Kelly had come out of her marriage with a child. He frowned, trying to remember the age of her daughter. For some reason, he couldn't recall Luke ever mentioning that she was pregnant or that she'd had a baby. He'd just one day mentioned Kelly's daughter as if the little girl had always existed.

He glanced in his rearview mirror, confirming that Ava was tuned in to her music and tuned out to everything else.

"She's tall for her age, isn't she?"

Kelly seemed surprised by the comment—and a little wary. "How old do you think she is?"

"Well, considering that you got married just over eleven years ago, I figured she couldn't be more than ten."

"That's a reasonable guess," Kelly agreed, without actually confirming the accuracy of it. But before he could question her further, she spoke again. "Lukas said that the house I'm renting is next door to Matthew's new place."

Jack nodded. "In fact, the house is owned by his mother-in-law, Charlotte Something-Something Branston."

"Something-Something?"

"There might be a few more 'somethings,'" he told her. "She's been married a few times."

"Where does she live?"

"Montana."

He smiled in response to her quizzical look. "Long story."

"It's a long drive," she reminded him.

She was right, and since talking about Matt and Georgia was easier than trying to manufacture another topic of conversation, he filled her in on some of the details.

"Georgia had three-year-old twins and was pregnant with her third child when her husband died, so Charlotte suggested that she leave Manhattan and move to Pinehurst to live with her. A few months after Pippa was born, Charlotte headed off to Vegas for a couple of weeks with some friends, fell in love with a cowboy from Montana, and married him. So Georgia was in an unfamiliar town and on her own now with three kids, and then Matt moved in next door."

"And the young mother suddenly had a white knight riding to her rescue," Kelly guessed.

"Actually, he's an orthopedic surgeon," Jack reminded her teasingly.

"But no one does the white-knight routine better than your big brother."

"True," he agreed. "But in this case, I think it might actually have been Georgia and her kids who saved him. Matt had a really hard time after the divorce."

Kelly's nod confirmed that she was aware of those details. "Sounds like Matt and Georgia were lucky to find one another, that each was exactly what the other was looking for, even if neither of them realized it."

"They do seem perfect for one another, and Matt absolutely dotes on her kids." Of course, Jack's oldest brother had always wanted a family of his own.

"He would," she agreed. "Although a lot of men wouldn't want to take on the responsibility of someone else's child."

He didn't miss that she'd said child and not children, and he suspected that she wasn't thinking of Matt and Georgia now but of another situation—possibly even her own. And he wondered if she spoke from experience, if she'd been alone since her divorce, reluctant to get involved again for fear that another man wouldn't accept her daughter.

But he didn't ask, because it was none of his business. They'd had a brief fling that was ancient history—he had no right to pry into her personal life now.

Except that the history between them continued to haunt his dreams, even after thirteen years. And even more so since he'd learned of her intention to return to Pinehurst.

He still didn't know what had precipitated the move, or what Kelly's daughter thought about her decision. He couldn't imagine that it was easy for a kid to be uprooted from everything that was familiar and moved clear across the country.

He glanced in the rearview mirror again. Kelly's daughter was a beautiful girl, with long, dark hair just like her mother—aside from the purple streaks, of course. Her eyes were a similar shape, too, and fringed with long, sooty lashes. But the color of her eyes was different. Kelly's eyes were the warm, golden color of aged whiskey; Ava's were a clear, emerald green.

He stole another glance, trying to figure out what it was about the child that made him uneasy.

"I guess Ava will be attending Parkdale," he said now.

"That's the plan," Kelly agreed. "I just hope she's lucky enough to make the kind of friends that I made at school there."

"It must have been difficult for her, leaving Seattle."

"It would have been more difficult if we'd stayed."

It was a surprising revelation from a woman who had previously volunteered no information about her reason for the move across the country. But she didn't say anything else, and though he was curious, he didn't press for any details.

Instead, as they passed the elementary school, he said, "You'll be happy to know that Mrs. Vanderheide finally retired a couple years ago."

She smiled. "That is good news—at least for Ava."

"And for all future generations of seventh graders," he agreed. "Which was proven by the fact that almost all of Pinehurst turned out for her retirement party at the school. She thought they were all there to celebrate her forty years of teaching, but I think everyone just wanted to make sure that she really was retiring."

The sensuous sound of her soft chuckle heated his blood.

Ancient history, he reminded himself again.

He tightened his grip on the steering wheel and turned onto Larkspur Drive, grateful the journey was almost at its end.

"This is it," he said, pulling into a wide asphalt driveway beside the two-story saltbox-style house. He noticed that there were lights on at both the front and back doors—

no doubt Matt's wife wanted the place to look warm and welcoming, and it did.

"Georgia said she would leave a key in the mailbox," he told Kelly now. "She also wanted you to know that they had a cleaning company come in yesterday to give the whole house a thorough once-over and that she was in today to inspect and put clean sheets on the beds."

"I'll have to remember to thank her for that," she said. "Because right now, I'm tired enough to fall face down on any horizontal surface."

He shifted into park and glanced in the rearview mirror again. "Apparently your daughter doesn't need to be horizontal."

Kelly turned to look at Ava, who had fallen asleep with her head against the window. Since the days when she could carry her slumbering child were likely long gone, he wasn't surprised when she reached back to tap the girl's shoulder. "Wake up, Ava. We're home."

He was surprised by her use of the word *home,* and he frowned as it echoed in his head. It seemed strange to him that, after being gone for more than fifteen years, Kelly would still refer to Pinehurst as home. He hadn't known if this was a temporary relocation or a permanent move, and he refused to admit that it mattered. He could have asked Luke, of course. No doubt his brother was privy to all of the details of her plans. But asking Luke anything about Kelly when he'd been so careful not to mention her name for so long would undoubtedly trigger more questions that Jack wasn't prepared to answer.

There was little he didn't share with his brothers, but the fact that he'd spent a wild weekend with Kelly Cooper was a secret he'd kept for thirteen years—and one that he had no intention of revealing now.

Chapter Two

While Kelly roused her daughter, Jack retrieved their luggage from the trunk. He took the suitcases upstairs, setting the one with Kelly's name on it in the biggest room and her daughter's in the room directly across the hall. A quick glance at the tag gave him pause.

He couldn't remember the name of the guy Kelly had married, but regardless of whether or not she'd taken his name, he would have expected their child to have it. But the tag read *Ava Cooper*—and it made him think again about the reasons for Kelly's divorce and her decision to move Ava so far away from Seattle.

Reminding himself that it was none of his business, he headed back down the stairs and, following the sound of voices, into the kitchen.

"You're only asking for mushrooms because you know I don't like them," Kelly said.

"I'm asking for mushrooms because I *do* like them and that's what I want on my pizza," her daughter insisted.

"Well, no one else does, so we're not getting them."

He knew he shouldn't get involved and he had no intention of staying, but Jack heard himself say, "I like mushrooms."

Ava looked at her mother, her smile more than a little smug. Kelly didn't look annoyed; she looked…unnerved. Which didn't make any sense to him at all.

"And bacon?" Ava queried.

"And bacon," he confirmed.

"Fine, I'll get half with bacon and mushrooms," Kelly relented. Then she looked at Jack. "Which means that you're staying for pizza."

"If you'd told me you were hungry, I could have stopped somewhere on the way from the airport," he told her.

"I didn't realize how hungry I was until now."

"Then you should order from Marco's—they deliver and they're quick."

He gave her the number, and while Kelly made the call, Ava ventured upstairs to check out her new room and start unpacking. After pizza was ordered, Kelly took a look around. She'd seen photos and even videos of the house before signing the lease, but she wanted to see everything up close. Jack opted to respond to some email messages on his BlackBerry while she explored.

She was back in less than ten minutes, and obviously pleased with everything she'd seen. "Lukas told me the place was furnished, but I didn't expect it to be so well equipped. There are pots and pans and dishes and cutlery in the kitchen—and even toilet paper in each of the bathrooms. Something else I'll have to thank Georgia for, because I didn't think to pack any of that in my suitcase."

"I'd be surprised if you had room," Jack said. "Considering that you each only brought one suitcase and one carry-on."

"I prefer to travel light, but there's a lot more to come. It just seemed easier—and cheaper—to ship the rest rather than pay the airline fees for extra baggage."

"Makes sense," he agreed.

But he still had questions about her sudden decision to return to Pinehurst after so many years away. And he had an uneasy suspicion that nagged at the back of his mind. He hadn't wanted to ask it while her daughter was in the backseat of his car—even if she had seemed oblivious to their discussion—but it was a question that needed an answer.

"I just hope it arrives on schedule," Kelly continued her explanation about the luggage. "Because my work clothes are in that shipment and I start my new job on the fifteenth."

"Was it the job that lured you back to Pinehurst?"

"It was the deciding factor, but I've been thinking about coming back for a while," she admitted. "I wanted a fresh start for Ava and myself."

Jack tipped her chin up, forcing her to meet his gaze.

The contact was casual, but he would have sworn that sparks flew at the brief touch of his fingertip against her skin. Judging by the way Kelly's eyes widened, she'd felt them, too.

He dropped his hand, forced himself to remember the question he needed to ask. "Was he abusive?"

She blinked, clearly startled by the inquiry. "What? Who?"

"Your ex-husband," he said. "Because I've been wracking my brain, and that's the only reason I could imagine for taking a child three thousand miles away from her father."

Kelly dropped her gaze and shook her head. "No, Malcolm wasn't abusive."

He wanted to feel relieved—he *was* relieved. And yet, he couldn't let go of the suspicion that there was something more Kelly wasn't telling him.

A suspicion that was confirmed when she looked up again and said, "And he wasn't Ava's father."

Kelly held her breath, waiting for Jackson's response to her revelation. But before he could say anything, the doorbell rang and Ava was racing down the stairs in response to the summons. "Pizza's here!"

And that quickly, any chance of taking the conversation further was gone.

Her daughter flung open the door without first looking through the peephole to confirm that it was their food delivery. Of course, in Seattle no one could gain access to their door without first being buzzed into the building, so now that things were different they would have to have a discussion about basic safety precautions.

Or maybe not, considering that this was Pinehurst, where many of the residents didn't even lock their doors during the day. And wasn't that one of the reasons she'd brought her daughter here? To give her the benefits of living in a small, close-knit community. Of course, an even bigger reason stood right beside her.

As it turned out, it wasn't their pizza at the door—it was Lukas with his arms full of grocery bags. Setting the bags down inside the door, he swept Ava up for a big hug. "There's my favorite girl."

The girl in question would have been absolutely mortified by such an overt display of affection from her mother, but her cherished "uncle" got away with a lot. And Kelly suspected that the prospect of living in close proximity to Lukas was the one reason that Ava hadn't kicked harder and screamed louder about the move.

He ruffled her hair. "What's with the purple streaks?"

"Mom wouldn't let me have a belly button ring."

"Makes perfect sense to me. And speaking of your mom…"

He turned to wrap his arms around Kelly, squeezing her so tight she could hardly breathe, but it felt so good—so right—to be in his arms that tears filled her eyes.

"I missed you," she told him now. "I never realize how much I miss you until I see you again."

"I'm just glad that you're finally home." He released her

with obvious reluctance and looked at his brother. "Thanks for doing the airport run."

"When have I ever objected to picking up a beautiful woman?" Jackson asked.

Lukas chuckled. "Never."

The knots in Kelly's stomach returned. Was Jackson's comment just brotherly banter or a statement to her—a reminder that she'd never meant anything more to him than any other casual pickup? And why did she even care? She hadn't come back to Pinehurst to rekindle her relationship with Jackson but for Ava to establish a relationship with her father.

Now his words gave Kelly pause. Was he still a relentless flirt and unrepentant playboy? Because that was hardly the type of male role model that she wanted for her impressionable daughter. Or was she just looking to find fault, to justify her own actions? Since that was a question she couldn't answer right now, she shifted her attention to Lukas instead.

"I should have figured you'd be here in time for pizza," she said, as the delivery car pulled up in front.

"Am I?" He turned to follow her gaze and grinned. "My timing is impeccable as usual."

As Kelly dug in her purse for money to pay for their dinner, she couldn't help thinking his timing would have been much better if he'd been able to meet them at the airport. But she could breathe a little easier now, confident that she'd survived her first face-to-face with Jackson relatively unscathed.

She knew they had to finish their interrupted conversation at some point, but not today. Not when her heart was already feeling battered and bruised by the callous remarks of a man who probably had no idea how much he could hurt her. Instead, she gestured for Jackson to follow Ava—and the pizza—into the kitchen.

He shook his head. "I need to get going."

"I thought you were going to stay for pizza," Kelly said.

"I've got files to review for court tomorrow."

Lukas retrieved the bags he'd dropped. "The files will still be there in half an hour," he pointed out to his brother.

"I'm sure you guys have lots to catch up on," Jackson said. "You don't need me hanging around."

"Your choice—and more pizza for me," Lukas said with a shrug and a grin as he headed toward the kitchen.

Kelly wished she could be so nonchalant, but she wasn't sure if she was relieved or disappointed that Jackson was leaving. She followed him to the door. "Thanks again for meeting us at the airport."

"It wasn't a problem," he assured her.

Her heart was pounding so hard and fast, she was surprised he couldn't hear it, and she had to moisten her suddenly dry lips before she could speak. "What I started to say, when we were in the kitchen, about Ava's father—"

"It's not really any of my business," he said.

Actually, it is, she wanted to respond. But aloud she only said, "I *want* to talk to you about it. There are some things you should know."

He frowned. "Do you have legal questions about custody?"

She wondered how he could be so oblivious—or maybe she expected too much of him. After thirteen years, he had no reason to suspect that she had news that would turn his whole life—*all of their lives*—upside down. And instead of being exasperated, maybe she should be grateful that he had no clue, because it meant that she could keep her secret a little bit longer.

Except that coming face-to-face with her daughter's

father, she was forced to acknowledge that thirteen years was already too long. Jackson needed to know the truth, and she needed to deal with the consequences of that revelation—whatever they might be.

"It's nothing like that," she said to him now. "I don't want to talk to you as a lawyer but as a...friend."

"Okay," he finally said. "Why don't you give me a call when you're ready to talk?"

If she waited until she was ready, she knew that the conversation might not happen for another thirteen years. But she nodded. "I will. Thanks."

"Okay," he said again, and then he was gone.

Kelly stood for a moment, staring at the back of the door and feeling much like she imagined Pandora had felt when she'd lifted the lid of a box that should never have been opened.

Lukas and Ava were both on their second slices of pizza by the time Kelly made her way to the kitchen. They also had cans of soda, which Lukas had obviously brought in one of the grocery bags. Beside Kelly's plate was an open bottle and a glass of her favorite Shiraz.

"Okay, you're forgiven for not meeting us at the airport."

He smiled. "I figured you'd had a long day and might need some help to unwind."

"Food and good company would have sufficed, but the wine is a definite bonus." She picked up the glass and sipped.

"Eat." He nudged her plate toward her. "If you drink that on an empty stomach, you'll fall asleep at the table."

Kelly dutifully picked up a slice of pizza and took a bite.

"I brought a few essentials for the morning, too," Lukas told her. "Bread, milk, eggs, juice, coffee."

"Coffee?" She nearly whimpered with gratitude. "Now you're definitely forgiven."

Ava polished off her third slice and wiped her fingers on a paper napkin. "Can I go now?"

"'Thanks for dinner, Mom,'" Kelly said, mimicking her daughter's voice. "'You're very welcome, honey.' 'May I be excused now?' 'Of course.'"

Lukas lifted his can of soda to hide his smile. Ava, predictably, rolled her eyes, before she dutifully intoned, "Thanks for dinner, Mom. May I be excused now?"

"Of course," Kelly said agreeably. "*After* you put your plate in the dishwasher."

Lukas reached for another slice as Ava clomped up the stairs. "So," he said, when she was out of earshot. "How does it feel to be back?"

"I'm not sure," she admitted. "It's been such a long time. I don't know if this is the right thing—for Ava or for me."

"She's not happy about the move?"

"That's the understatement of the year."

He shrugged. "She's twelve. She'll get over it."

"I hope so."

"So—belly button ring?" he prompted.

She just shook her head. "Can you believe it?"

"I'm having a little difficulty reconciling my memories of the cute little second-grader who clutched my hand so tightly with the brooding purple-haired preteen-ager who barely looked up from her plate."

"The purple streaks aren't so bad. You should have seen her a few months ago—her hair was Pepto-Bismol pink. Her best friend's older sister put the color on for her one afternoon when I had to work late." She sighed. "The first tangible evidence that my formerly docile angel had developed a rebellious streak."

Lukas winced sympathetically. "How did you handle that?"

"I took a deep breath and reminded myself that hair color is easily undone—unlike a piercing or a tattoo. And I knew that it was, at least in part, my fault. I'd been so preoccupied with my job that I didn't realize how much distance had grown between us," she admitted.

"When rumors of cutbacks first started circulating around the lunchroom at work, I crossed my fingers and prayed that I wouldn't lose my job. And when those cuts were made and I was spared, I was so grateful I didn't balk at all the extra hours I had to work.

"And then I realized that I'd given up my life to keep my job. And I'd somehow lost the close connection I used to share with Ava." Her daughter's recent willful behavior was proof of that—and reminded Kelly uncomfortably of the impulsiveness that she herself had occasionally exhibited before motherhood had taught her to consider the consequences of her actions.

"And because I was working so many extra hours," she continued her explanation, "Ava was hanging around with her friend Rachel—and Regan, Rachel's sixteen-year-old sister—a lot."

"Then I'd guess that you made this move at the right time."

"I hope so," she said again.

"What aren't you telling me?"

Kelly lifted her glass and took another sip of wine as she considered how much she should say.

"Because I know there's more to this cross-country move than that," he prompted when she failed to respond.

She nodded. "I wanted a career change and a change of scenery for Ava, but I also hoped that coming back to Pinehurst might provide a chance for her to meet her father."

His brows rose. "Then he does live in Pinehurst."

"He does live in Pinehurst," she confirmed.

"Someone I know?" he asked.

The undercurrents in his tone were exactly why she'd never revealed the identity of her daughter's father to him. "Doesn't everyone know almost everyone else in this town?" she countered.

"Who is it?"

She touched a hand to his arm. "Please—let me tell him before I tell you."

He frowned. "Are you saying that this guy doesn't know he has a twelve-year-old daughter?"

"I couldn't tell him," she reminded Lukas. "By the time I knew I was pregnant, he was already with someone else."

She'd wanted to tell Jackson that she was going to have his baby. Although she'd had no expectations of a future for them together when he'd left Chicago, she'd hoped that the revelation of her pregnancy would make him want to be a father to their child. But as much as she didn't want to do it alone, she'd had no doubt—even then—that she was going to keep her baby.

Except that when she'd finally gotten up the nerve to call, he'd told her that he was once again engaged to Sara Ross—the daughter of one of the senior partners at his firm. And while Kelly didn't believe he would get married solely for the purpose of advancing his career, she didn't doubt that dumping the boss's daughter would jeopardize his future at the firm. And nothing had mattered to Jackson as much as his career. So she'd only offered congratulations and ended the call with her heart in pieces and the news of her pregnancy unrevealed.

"Yeah, you told me what happened," Lukas admitted now. "But you didn't tell me who the father was."

"No, I didn't," she agreed. "And I'm not going to tell you now. Not until I've told him."

She could tell by the muscle that clenched in his jaw that Lukas wasn't finished with his interrogation, but she also knew he wouldn't press for more details. At least not yet.

Jack was distracted, and he'd never been the type to let anything—or *anyone*—interfere with his concentration, especially when it came to his work. He was a well-respected and generously compensated family law attorney because he was diligent and focused. He paid attention to details and he made every client feel as if his or her case was the only one that mattered.

And yet, in the middle of a cross-examination during a custody hearing that morning, he'd actually lost his train of thought. Sure, he'd recovered fairly quickly, and it didn't seem as if anyone else in the courtroom had even noticed that he'd faltered. But he'd noticed. And he knew that it was Kelly Cooper's fault.

"Hello, Jackson."

He blinked, half-suspecting that her appearance in the open doorway of his office was an illusion, and more than half-hoping that she would disappear again. But when he opened his eyes, she was still there—and looking even hotter than the woman who had starred in his dreams the night before. And the night before that. In fact, every one of the five nights that had passed since she'd come back to Pinehurst.

She made her way across the carpet, putting one sexy foot in front of the other in the way that women had perfected to make their hips sway and men drool. And as much as he wished it weren't true, he was very close to drooling.

Damn, she looked spectacular. In the slim-fitting burgundy skirt, silky white V-neck blouse and peep-toe shoes that added close to three inches to her five-foot-seven-inch frame, she looked professional, confident—and dangerous.

He frowned at the thought, but he couldn't deny it was true. For too many years, Kelly Cooper had threatened his peace of mind. It had been easy enough to ignore the girl next door when she was a kid. Then adolescence had turned her bony, sticklike figure into a woman's body with subtle but undeniable curves. And he'd started to have very inappropriate fantasies about his little brother's best friend. Thankfully, he'd gone away to school and had managed to put her out of his mind. Mostly.

"You told me to call you, but you haven't returned any of my calls. I was beginning to think I would have to schedule an appointment to see you."

"I'm not hard to find, but I am busy," he said pointedly.

"I can appreciate that," she said. "And I promise you, I wouldn't be here if it wasn't important."

"How did you get past my secretary?" Colleen was usually a pit bull when it came to protecting her boss's time and space.

Kelly just smiled. "Your secretary was my eleventh-grade lab partner."

Having lived in Pinehurst his whole life, he understood that personal connections frequently trumped protocol. "Okay, that answers the how," he admitted. "But not the why."

She settled into one of the client chairs on the other side of his desk, and crossed one long, shapely leg over the other. "I just wanted to talk to you without my daughter or your brother interrupting, so I asked Colleen if she could squeeze me into your appointment schedule."

"Now you've stirred my curiosity," he admitted. And certain other areas as well.

"Your brother was, and still is, my best friend," she reminded him. "And while you and I were never close friends, we used to be friendly. And then, for one incredible weekend, we were a lot more."

Whatever he'd expected when she'd walked through his door, it wasn't a walk down memory lane. Not that he was unwilling to take the journey, but he knew it was unwise. His past with Kelly was the past—no way would he risk starting anything up again with his brother living in the same town. Luke had always been protective of his friend and if he ever suspected that Jack had been naked with Kelly—well, Jack didn't even want to think about what he might do. It was smarter, and safer, to keep the past in the past. "Why are you bringing this up now?"

"Because I'm hoping, now that I'm living in Pinehurst again, that we can get back to being friendly."

"Have I been unfriendly?"

"Not exactly," she admitted. "You've been…distant."

"I've been busy," he said again.

"Your brother and sister-in-law invited Ava and I over for burgers last night and while we were there, one of Georgia's sons asked Matthew why 'Uncle Jack' hasn't been around to visit in so long. Matt told him you had a big court case coming up, but the way he looked at me before he responded made me think he was making excuses."

"He wasn't."

"I don't want you to feel uncomfortable visiting your brother and his family just because I'm living next door."

"I don't."

She shifted forward in her chair, enough so that he could see the slightest hint of cleavage in the V-neck of her blouse. "You're not worried that the chemistry that exploded between us thirteen years ago might still be simmering?"

"No," he lied.

"Well, that's good then," she said, but her easy smile didn't reach her eyes.

"Thirteen years is a long time," he said, in an attempt to convince himself as much as her.

She nodded. "It always boggled my mind that I could be such good friends with Lukas, that I could snuggle up with him to watch a movie, hold his hand as a gesture of comfort or support, and never feel anything remotely like the zing that I felt whenever I was in the same room with you."

"Chemistry is a personal thing," he noted.

She tilted her head to look up at him. "Have you ever felt that zing with anyone else?"

"Too many times to count," he lied.

She seemed disappointed—and maybe even a little hurt—by his casual response. But Kelly being Kelly, she didn't try to deny her feelings or hide behind a flippant response. She was, as always, brutally and painfully honest.

"I haven't," she told him. "From the first time you kissed me, on my sixteenth birthday, I've never felt that zing with anyone else."

"Not even your husband?" he challenged.

She shook her head. "No, not with anyone else."

Knowing how incredibly passionate she was, he was surprised that she would settle for comfort and companionship. On the other hand, it might explain why her marriage had failed.

"I think you're romanticizing the memory," he told her.

"Maybe," she allowed. "But it wasn't my first kiss. And you weren't my first lover—but you're the one I've never forgotten."

Even if what she was saying was true, he wouldn't let it matter. Because rekindling a romantic relationship with Kelly wasn't an option. Getting involved with a woman who was also his brother's best friend could only lead to a whole lot of grief, not to mention the fact that she had a kid to think about.

So instead of admitting that he'd never forgotten her either, he only said, "Is there a purpose to this reminiscence?"

"I wanted you to know that I had some concerns about coming back to Pinehurst now."

"Because of what happened between us so many years ago?" he asked skeptically.

Her smile was sad. "Is that so unbelievable?"

"Yes," he said.

"Did you never think of me after that weekend?"

"Sure," he said easily. "But I didn't think that one weekend changed anything."

"It changed everything—at least for me," she told him. "But when I called, you were already back together with Sara."

"It's not like you called a few days later," he felt compelled to point out in his own defense. "It was more like a few months."

Actually, two months, three weeks and five days, and during that time, not a single day had gone by in which he hadn't picked up the phone to call her. But he'd never actually dialed her number, because he knew it would be a mistake. Because after only three days with her, he'd known that he could fall fast and hard for Kelly Cooper, and that was a complication neither of them needed at that point in their lives.

She nodded in acknowledgment. "I know."

"And Sara and I had a history together," he continued. "So when she said she'd made a mistake in ending our engagement, I agreed that we should try to work things out."

"Because you loved her," she said softly. "And I was

just the girl who helped you forget—for a few days—that she'd broken your heart."

He heard the vulnerability in her tone and he knew that, even after so many years, his reconciliation had hurt her. But the truth was, he'd never thought about Sara—not once—throughout the weekend that he was with Kelly. So instead of nodding and letting her believe it was true, he said, "I wanted you to believe that."

She frowned at his admission. "Why?"

"Because we'd both agreed, at the end of the weekend that we'd spent together, that it couldn't ever happen again. And then you called, and I could hear in your voice that you'd changed your mind, that you wanted more." And in that moment, as much as he'd wanted *her*, he knew there could be no future for them together. Not at that time and definitely not in light of the conversation he'd had with his brother.

"And you didn't want more," she guessed. "Not with me."

"What I wanted didn't matter," he told her. "You were still in school and barely twenty-one years old."

"You're right—I was twenty-one years old." She paused to draw in a deep breath before looking up at him. "And I was pregnant."

Chapter Three

Jackson stared at her for a long moment, as if he couldn't quite comprehend what she was telling him. When he finally spoke, his tone conveyed as much confusion as his words. "You were…pregnant?"

She nodded.

He frowned but didn't say anything else.

"On the way from the airport, you asked how old Ava was. She turned twelve in February."

"Are you saying…?" His question trailed off, as if he couldn't bear to speak the words out loud and acknowledge the possibility.

But Kelly had been holding on to the secret for too many years and she wasn't going to hide the truth for even a minute longer. "She's your daughter."

His mouth snapped shut; his face actually paled. But after another pause, which was probably only a few seconds but felt like hours, his gaze narrowed and he shook his head. "Nice try, Kelly."

She felt her back go up. "What is it you think I'm trying to do?"

"Suck me into paying twelve years of child support."

"Child support?"

"I know you came back here to work at Richmond Pharmaceuticals, but losing your job in Seattle must have—"

"I *chose* to leave my job in Seattle," she interjected.

He shrugged. "Regardless of the reason for your financial difficulties—"

She couldn't help but laugh at the absurdity of his allegation. Because the truth was, between the inheritance left to Kelly by her grandmother and the trust set up for Ava by her former step-grandmother, she had no immediate financial issues. "You really think this is about money?"

"I can't imagine any other reason that you would concoct such an outrageous story."

"Maybe it seems outrageous to you," she acknowledged. "But it's not a story—it's the truth."

He snorted derisively. "Are you willing to submit your daughter to DNA testing to prove it?"

"Absolutely."

Her immediate and unequivocal response finally seemed to give him pause.

"Trust me, Jack, if I got to choose a father for my daughter, I wouldn't have chosen someone who's made it more than clear that he doesn't want to be a father."

He considered that for a moment, then asked, "You really do think I'm her father?"

"You really think I had so many lovers I don't know who fathered my child?"

"I wasn't your first," he said, in an echo of her own statement.

"No," she agreed. She hadn't been innocent, but she had been inexperienced. "You were my second."

He winced. "How the hell was I supposed to know something like that?"

"You weren't," she admitted. In fact, she'd done everything she could to ensure he didn't know. Afraid that her naïveté might put him off, she'd tried to make up for her lack of experience with enthusiasm. She'd been in love with him for so long, nothing had mattered to Kelly except that she was finally going to be with him.

"You told me you were on the pill," he said now.

"No." She felt her cheeks flush at the memory of that awkward conversation. "When the condom broke, you asked if I was 'safe' and I said yes."

"But you weren't," he said accusingly.

"I thought you were talking about the risk of sexually transmitted diseases."

Jack scrubbed a hand over his face. "It would have been nice to have clarified that little misunderstanding thirteen years ago."

"I was young and naive, but even if I could, I wouldn't change anything that happened back then because it gave me my daughter."

"Except that you're now claiming she's my daughter, too."

She should have known this would be a mistake. She'd suspected that he would be shocked, and probably more than a little angry. But his disbelief cut her to the quick. She had *never* slept around and there was *no* possibility that anyone else was the father of her child.

Of course, Jack had no way of knowing that—especially considering that she'd had no direct contact with him over the past thirteen years. But that didn't make his accusation hurt any less. She stood up. "I thought you had a right to know. I thought *Ava* had a right to know. But I'd rather she didn't know the identity of her father than to know that he doesn't want to be her father."

"*If* I am her father—"

Kelly cut him off with a sharp expletive and turned away, but not before he saw her eyes fill with tears.

Jack tried to ignore the twist of guilt. He hadn't barged into her place of work with outrageous accusations. Why should he feel guilty just because he wasn't willing to accept her claim unequivocally? Well, he wasn't. He had questions, and he damn well wanted answers to those questions.

And now she was just going to walk out?

The phone on his desk buzzed. "Donald Winter is here for his two-thirty appointment," Colleen announced.

He pushed away from his desk as Kelly reached for the handle of the door. "Wait."

"No." She shook her head, refusing to look at him. "I'm done here."

He slapped his hand against the frame. "You can't drop a bombshell like that and just walk out."

"You have a client waiting," she reminded him.

But right now, Donald Winter and his legal issues were the least of Jack's concerns. In fact, standing so close to Kelly, breathing in her hauntingly familiar scent, he could barely remember the client's name. He tried to focus his thoughts on the here and now, on Kelly's revelation and his response to it. But memories of that one long-ago weekend teased the back of his mind, and he felt something begin to stir low in his belly.

He dropped his hand from the door, curled his fingers into his palms so that he didn't give in to the urge to touch her. Because he'd lied. When she'd asked if he'd ever felt the same zing with anyone else, he'd blatantly and unapologetically lied. It was true that he'd been attracted to other women—probably too many other women—but never had he experienced an attraction as compelling or intense as his desire for Kelly.

Even now, even when she was making wild accusations that could turn his entire life upside down, he couldn't ignore the heat thrumming in his veins. And because he was standing so close to her, he could see the pulse point pounding at the base of her jaw, and he knew that she was feeling that zing, too.

"The client can wait," he said to her now.

She finally looked at him, and he was relieved to see that her golden eyes were clear again, with no hint of the tears that had twisted knots in his belly. "There's no reason to make him wait—we're done here."

"We're not even close to being done."

"I said everything I wanted to say and you've made your feelings on the subject more than clear."

"Dammit, Kelly, I don't know what I'm feeling," he admitted. "But as an attorney, I'm finding it difficult to accept the word of a former lover without any concrete proof when I know there's no way in hell I would let any client of mine do the same."

"We used to be more than lovers, Jack. We used to be friends."

"We used to be," he agreed. "But I haven't heard a single word from you in thirteen years."

"Why would I lie about something that is as easy to disprove as it is to prove?" she challenged.

It was a good question, and one he probably should have considered. But his mind had been reeling since he'd heard her say "I was pregnant"—and frantically trying to reject the possibility that her child could be his.

Because kids weren't anywhere in his plan. Sure, he'd considered the possibility when he was married, but when his marriage had fallen apart, so had the expectation that he would someday have a family. Now Kelly wanted him to believe that he was the father of her twelve-year-old child? His brain simply refused to wrap around the possibility.

"So you really want to do a DNA test?" he asked her now.

"No," she said. "What I really want—and probably what

you want, too—is to forget we ever had this conversation. Unfortunately, I know that's not going to happen."

He shook his head. "No, it's not. And if—"

Her steely glare had him biting back the words and frantically seeking another direction for his thoughts.

"*If* you have some time tonight," he said quickly, "I could stop by and we could discuss this in more detail."

She shook her head. "I'm not talking about any of this around my daughter."

"Don't you mean *our* daughter?" he challenged.

"Make up your mind, Jackson. You can't deny paternity in one breath and use it as a weapon in the next."

"I just want the truth."

"And you need a DNA test for that? Did you even look at her?"

"She looks like you," he said dismissively.

And though it was undeniably true, there was something about the girl that had—even at a first glance—nagged at him. "If that's all you saw, maybe that's all anyone else will see," she said.

"So you're just going to walk away?"

"I told you, Jacks—I thought you had a right to know. But I have no desire to force you into a role you don't want to fill."

"You can't blame me for being suspicious," he said. "It's my job to ask the tough questions."

"And you've obviously done well enough at your job to get your name on the door," she noted. "Or was that a wedding present?"

His gaze narrowed. "I don't remember you having a nasty streak."

"We spent three days together more than thirteen years ago—there were a lot of things you didn't know, never mind remember."

And then she yanked open the door and walked out.

* * *

Jack met with Donald Winter, but he cancelled the rest of his afternoon appointments after that. Actually, he told Colleen to cancel his appointments on account of a family emergency—a request that had her jaw falling open. Because Jack Garrett never cancelled appointments for any kind of personal reasons, because nothing had ever mattered more to him than his career. But right now, he couldn't focus on anyone else's legal problems. He couldn't think at all with Kelly's words still ringing in his ears.

She's your daughter.

He still had trouble believing it could be true. And yet, as much as he wanted to continue to deny even the possibility, deep in his heart he knew Kelly wouldn't lie about something so monumental. Nor would she have made the claim unless she was one-hundred-percent convinced that it was true.

Which meant—Lord help him!—that he was the father of Kelly's daughter. He had a daughter. And not a chubby-cheeked infant or even a wide-eyed toddler but a twelve-year-old. For God's sake, the kid was practically a teenager!

And to Jack's mind, that was definitely a family emergency.

When he left the office, he did so without any kind of plan. He only knew that he needed some time and space, so he got into his car and drove. Since the death of his parents, family had been himself and his two brothers. Now that Matt was married to Georgia, that family had grown to include his new sister-in-law and her three children. And considering that Luke was a lot like Matt with respect to his ideals about hearth and home, Jack figured his younger brother would also hook up with one woman and have a family of his own someday.

But that wasn't Jack's future. When his marriage ended,

he figured any chance of someday having a family had ended with it. And truthfully, he hadn't been too disappointed. The whole wife-and-kids thing had never been his life's ambition. But now it seemed he had a kid, whether he wanted one or not. And right now, he was leaning in the direction of "not." He wasn't proud to admit it, and he knew it wasn't what Kelly wanted to hear, but it was true. He was thirty-seven years old, content with his life. Adding a child to the mix now would turn everything upside down.

Not that it was his choice to make. The fact of Ava's paternity wasn't something that could be debated. A test would either prove that he was her father or—dammit, he knew there wasn't any "or." In his gut, he knew that Kelly was telling the truth. The fact that she hadn't faltered or flinched when he'd demanded proof of paternity convinced him that she had absolutely no doubt that he was the father of her child. Which meant that he had to accept not just the possibility but the probability that her twelve-year-old daughter was also his daughter.

He knew his responsibilities, at least in so far as the law was concerned. Despite Kelly's claim that she didn't want financial support, he understood that a father had a legal obligation to contribute toward his child's maintenance— to ensure that she had food, clothing and shelter. And he would do so.

It was his rights more than his responsibilities that gave him pause. He was more than willing to write checks, but did he want to play any more of a role in the child's life beyond that?

His practice in the field of family law had demonstrated to him time and time again that some people instinctively knew what it took to be good parents, and some people didn't. And he'd often wished that those who didn't would realize it before they made the mistake of procreating.

His brother, Matt, had always wanted to be a father, and when his girlfriend of only a few weeks told him she was pregnant, he hadn't hesitated to marry her. He'd been a doting husband, catering to Lindsay's every want and need—and thrilled beyond belief when Liam was born. Three years later, Lindsay admitted that Liam wasn't really Matt's son, that she'd already been pregnant when she seduced him. She'd chosen Matt because she knew he would want to be a father to her child, but once Liam's real father was back in the picture, she wanted to be with him. Considering his brother's experience, was it any wonder Jack was skeptical of Kelly's claim?

Not that the experience had sidetracked Matt from his ultimate goal of having a family of his own. Not for too long anyway. Once he got over Lindsay's betrayal and the loss of his son, he'd jumped with both feet into a relationship with his beautiful neighbor—a widow with three kids. In fact, Jack had stood up for Matt at his wedding to Georgia only a few weeks earlier, and though Shane and Quinn and Pippa weren't Matt's biological children, Jack knew his brother couldn't love those kids any more if they were.

Which only proved to Jack how different he was from his brother. When faced with the news that he was a father, he didn't feel the least bit paternal, just panicked. After his divorce, he'd accepted that fatherhood wasn't in the cards for him and moved on. And he'd felt no twinges of loss or regret. In fact, he'd been grateful that he and Sara hadn't had any children to fight over during the divorce. Not that they'd fought over much of anything. By the time she'd filed for divorce, it was obvious to both of them that whatever passion they'd once shared had long since burned out. Neither of them cared enough to take issue over anything.

Before she moved out, Sara had accused him of being cold and unfeeling, and Jack had accepted that she might be right. He figured the numbness was a natural consequence of having been witness to the breakdown of so many marriages and the nastiness that often accompanied the splits. Except that he only had to spend five minutes with Kelly Cooper to be feeling all kinds of emotions he didn't want to feel.

But the one that rose above all others, at least right now, was anger. He was furious that she hadn't made any effort to contact him at all over the past thirteen years. He'd been divorced for more than eight years and he was sure Luke would have advised her of the fact. Not because he suspected the news would have any significance to her, but just because he told her pretty much everything. But Kelly still hadn't initiated any contact. She hadn't even called to tell him that she was planning to move back to Pinehurst. And though it was a free country and she certainly didn't need his permission to change her residence, it would have been nice if she'd given him some kind of heads-up that she was planning to turn his entire world upside down.

He'd actually worried that she'd moved halfway across the country because of difficulties with her ex-husband. He'd assumed that she had some reason for taking her daughter away from her father. Now he learned that she was actually moving the child *to* her father. *Him.*

He yanked at his tie, unfastened the button at his throat.

He hadn't paid too much attention to Kelly's daughter when he'd met them at the airport. In fact, he'd tried not to pay too much attention to Kelly, either. He'd only been there because Lukas had asked him for a favor. But he had noticed—it was impossible not to notice—how much the girl looked like her mother.

She had the same willowy build, the same dark hair. But even when he was trying not to notice, the daughter's eyes had nagged at him. The shape and color of her eyes was

very similar to Lukas's—a coincidence that he'd immediately disregarded because the idea of Kelly and Lukas in a
romantic relationship was one he didn't like to contemplate.

He hadn't thought about the fact that his brother's eyes
were very much like his own, which meant that the child's
eyes were like his own. But apparently, even at that first
meeting, his subconscious had recognized the possibility
his mind still didn't want to acknowledge.

And he knew now that his life was never going to be
the same.

Kelly had expected to feel relieved after telling Jackson about Ava, but when she left his office, she was more
angry than anything else. She was hurt by his accusations,
infuriated by his questions. She wanted to rant and scream,
except there was no one she could rant to or scream at.
Desperate for an outlet for her turbulent emotions, she decided to clean.

Despite the fact that she and Ava had moved in less than
a week earlier, she attacked the furniture with a polishing
cloth and an enthusiasm born of anger and frustration. Dust
was viciously annihilated, smudges ruthlessly obliterated,
but nothing wiped the memory of Jack's skepticism from
her aching heart.

She plugged in the vacuum and turned her attention—
and fury—to the carpets, hopeful that the whirring of the
motor might drown out the thoughts in her head. And she
nearly jumped out of her skin when a hand came down on
her shoulder.

She stepped on the power button and pressed a shaky
palm to her heart. "Lukas—you nearly gave me a heart
attack."

"I called out, but you obviously didn't hear me."

"Obviously." She tucked a stray hair behind her ear. "What are you doing here?"

"You're not happy to see me?" he teased.

"I'm always happy to see you. I was just wondering why you stopped by."

"Because I can—because you're no longer three thousand miles away."

She managed a smile, but he frowned and touched a fingertip to the shadows beneath her eyes. "What's going on with you?"

"I'm just tired," she hedged. "I've been going nonstop over the past few weeks, in preparation for the move, and I haven't really had a chance to catch my breath."

"So put the vacuum away and give yourself a break," he suggested.

"I wanted to get this done before Ava came home," she said, but tucked the vacuum into the corner.

"Where is she?"

"She went to the park with Georgia and the kids." Kelly led the way to the kitchen, set up the coffee maker to brew a fresh pot.

"She must really be bored if she's hanging out with a couple of four-year-olds," Lukas noted, following her out to the back deck.

"She gets a kick out of the twins—and she absolutely adores Pippa."

"Typical only child," Lukas noted, settling into the Adirondack chair beside her. "If she had brothers and sisters of her own, she wouldn't be nearly as tolerant."

"Probably," she agreed. "But not something I have to worry about."

"But you're worried about something," he guessed.

She traced a finger over a knot in the wooden arm, avoiding his gaze.

"What's going on, Kel?"

"Can we just chalk it up to a really bad day?"

"Do you want to tell me about it?"

She did, but she couldn't. She shook her head.

Lukas frowned. "How is it that you talked to me more when you were living on the other side of the country?"

"I know there isn't anything I can't talk to you about—except this."

"Then it's about Ava's father," he guessed.

She hesitated, then nodded.

"You've seen him?" Lukas pressed.

She nodded again.

"Did you tell him?"

"I told him," she admitted. "And he didn't believe me."

His hands curled into fists on the arms of the chair. "Do you want me to talk to him?"

Kelly reached over and covered his fisted hand with her own. "Thanks, but I don't think that would help."

"What about Jack?"

Her breath caught in her throat. "What about Jack?"

"Why don't you talk to him?" Lukas suggested. "He could outline your legal options, suggest a course of action."

She shook her head, let her hand drop away. "Talking to Jack is not going to fix any of this."

"He's good at his job, Kel. He could—"

"No!" Her response was a little too vehement, a little too loud, and she winced even before Lukas frowned.

She pushed up from her chair, walked across the deck and tried to figure out a way to untangle the mess that she'd made. She wanted to tell Lukas everything, but it was harder than she'd imagined to find the words to reveal a secret that she'd kept closely guarded for so long. Especially when Jackson didn't believe it was true.

She should have been prepared for his questions, braced for his skepticism. But aside from having paternity results in hand, she didn't know what she could have said or done to convince him. And she wasn't going to pretend that he wasn't Ava's father just because he didn't want to be.

Because the simple truth that she'd learned from her visit to Jackson's office was that he didn't want to be a father—at least not to her daughter. Just like her mother and father hadn't wanted to be parents to Kelly. And Jackson's disinterest hurt more than his disbelief. He had every right to be angry with Kelly, but he had no reason to reject the daughter he didn't even know.

"Kelly?" Lukas prompted.

And she found herself trying to guess how he might react to the news—if Lukas would refuse to believe that Jackson was Ava's father, too. She didn't think she could bear it if he questioned the veracity of her claim. But even if he did believe her, he would be hurt by her silence, by her deception.

"I've made a mess of everything," she admitted softly.

She'd thought she was doing the right thing, but really, what had she known? She'd been twenty-one years old, pregnant and in love with her child's father, who was planning to marry someone else. Not the ideal scenario in which to make any kind of life-altering decision. But what alternative did she have? Because as scared as she was to have a baby on her own, she'd had too much pride to want to be with someone who didn't want to be with her.

Pride goes before a fall, her grandmother had been fond of saying. And Kelly knew that her actions in this situation might prove that adage to be true, especially if the decision she'd made ended up ruining her friendship with the one man who had always stood by her.

But even if she could turn back time, she didn't know that there was anything she would have done differently. Jackson had been in love with Sara. She didn't know any of the details of how or why their marriage failed, but she knew that he would never have made plans to marry her if he didn't love her. He and Kelly, on the other hand, had never made any plans.

She certainly hadn't planned to get pregnant, and she had no intention of using her baby to trap him. But she knew him well enough to know that if she'd told him she was pregnant, he would have broken off his relationship with Sara to marry her. He would have done "the right thing"—and he would have hated her for it. And that's why she'd never told him about the baby.

He hated her now, anyway, and she knew that was probably no less than she deserved. She only hoped she could somehow get through this without Lukas hating her, too.

When she heard the doorbell ring, she jumped at the reprieve, grateful for the interruption. Grateful for any excuse to escape Lukas's scrutiny and the inevitable confrontation that would follow her revelation.

Of course, that was before she opened the front door and found his brother standing on her porch.

She didn't realize Lukas had followed her to the door until he said, "Speak of the devil."

"Lukas." Jackson seemed even more surprised to see his brother than Kelly had been to see him at the door.

He glanced at her, a silent but desperate plea for help. But she didn't know what to say or do to extricate them from the suddenly awkward situation.

In that brief moment of charged silence, Lukas's gaze

bounced from Jackson to Kelly and back again. And Kelly knew the exact moment when all of the pieces clicked into place for him because he said, "You sonofabitch."

And then he hauled back a fist and punched his brother.

Chapter Four

Jackson's head snapped back; he stumbled.

"Lukas!" Kelly grabbed his arm as he advanced toward his brother again. "Stop!"

He turned around, so abruptly and with so much fury in his eyes that she took an instinctive step in retreat. "Goddammit, Kelly. My own brother?"

Her eyes filled with tears. "Let me explain."

But he shook his head and turned away.

A few seconds later, the back door slammed and she felt a single tear slide down her cheek.

"I wouldn't mind hearing that explanation," Jackson said.

She swiped impatiently at the trail of moisture and turned back to face him. The pithy response she'd intended died on her lips when she saw the red mark on his jaw. "Let's get you some ice," she said instead.

Jackson followed her through to the kitchen and took a seat at the kitchen table while she rummaged through the freezer.

"I told you that I didn't want you coming here," she reminded him.

"And I decided that you've been calling all the shots for too long."

She wrapped a bag of frozen peas in a clean tea towel and handed it to him. "How did that work out for you?"

He wiggled his jaw, winced. "Well, I didn't anticipate

getting sucker punched by my brother," he admitted, lifting the ice pack to his face. "And I didn't realize he had such a strong right hook."

"You haven't ever been on the receiving end before?"

"Not since we were kids."

The coffee that she'd put on for Lukas had finished brewing, so she poured two mugs and set one on the table in front of him. "I'm sorry. The last thing I ever wanted to do was to cause trouble between you and your brother."

The uninjured side of his mouth tipped up in a half-smile. "I knew you were going to be trouble for me the summer you turned sixteen."

She poured milk into her own coffee, and tried not to remember that summer. Or the fact that she'd fallen head over heels in love with Jackson Garrett the night of her sixteenth birthday when he'd kissed her for the first time.

She'd been so young, so naive. Of course, sixteen was only four years older than her daughter was right now—a reminder that brought her firmly back to the present.

"Why are you here, Jacks? Because I doubt very much you came over to take a stroll down memory lane."

"I blocked a lot of memories," he told her now. "Or tried to—until you showed up at my office today."

"I know I dropped a lot on you—I expected you'd need some time to think about things."

"I've done nothing but think since you left my office," he told her.

She wrapped her hands around her own mug of coffee.

"My head is still reeling," he continued.

She nodded.

"But I realize, in retrospect, maybe I didn't handle it as well as I could have."

"Maybe I didn't, either," she admitted. "Ava had an appointment with Dr. Turcotte this afternoon."

"Is she sick?"

"No, she's fine. I wanted her to have a complete checkup before she started school, anyway, and I asked the doctor, as part of his exam, to take a DNA swab."

"I feel like I should say that it isn't necessary."

"But it is." She met his gaze evenly. "I understand why you want proof. I might not like it, but I understand. And maybe when you have the results, you can let me know what you want to do."

Before showing up at Kelly's door, Jack had driven aimlessly around town for more than two hours, trying to figure out what he wanted to do, and he still didn't have any answers. The only thing he'd known for certain was that he needed to see Kelly—and her daughter. "Is…she here?"

"She?" Her brows lifted. "Do you mean Ava?"

He nodded.

"No, she isn't."

Jack was both relieved and disappointed. Part of the reason he'd steered toward Kelly's house was to see her daughter, because he thought that if he saw her again, he would know. The instinctive sense of relief warned that he wasn't yet ready to know.

"Is she still upset about the move?"

"Well, she only told me she hates it here four times today—it was seven yesterday."

"Sounds like progress."

"Monday will be the real test," she admitted. "That's when I start my new job."

"Is she old enough to be home by herself?" he asked.

"Technically, yes. But it's a new home, in a new neighborhood, so I decided it would be easier for both of us if I enrolled her in camp."

"Isn't she a little old for camp?"

"It's a junior leadership camp designed for kids entering grades seven and eight. It promotes goal setting and peer mentoring, and uses role playing to demonstrate responsible decision-making and leadership."

"What does something like that cost?"

"Is it always about money with you, Jackson?"

He turned over the ice pack, reapplied it to his jaw. "I was just curious."

"Don't worry—I'm not asking you to pay half."

"Does your ex-husband pay support?"

"He's not Ava's father," she reminded him.

"But if he acted *in loco parentis*—"

"He didn't. Malcolm was always very clear about the fact that Ava was *my* daughter. She grew up calling him 'Daddy' but she knew he wasn't really her father."

He frowned at that. "Has he had any contact with her since the divorce?"

"Ava," Kelly reminded him again.

"I know her name."

"Then why don't you say it? Does referring to her by pronouns make it easier to keep her at a distance?"

He scowled, because that was exactly what he'd been doing, even if he hadn't realized it. "Has your ex had any contact with *Ava* since the divorce?"

"She used to see him on a fairly regular basis at his mother's house, but she hasn't seen him at all since Bev died, more than three years ago. Since then, it's just been the two of us." She got up to refill her mug, topped up his, too. "That's one of the reasons I wanted to come home— back to Pinehurst. So that Ava could know her family." She looked across the table at him. "So she could know her father."

"You're not sick, are you?"

Her brow furrowed. "What?"

"Wasn't there a movie where the mother tracks down the father of her child because she's dying?"

"I'm not dying," Kelly assured him. "And even if I was, guardianship arrangements for Ava are set out in my will."

"Lukas," he guessed.

She just nodded, and he tried not to be annoyed that she would entrust her daughter to the care of his brother when she hadn't even trusted him with the information that he was her daughter's father.

"You'll change that if the test results prove that I'm her father," he said.

"*When* the test results confirm paternity, it won't be necessary to change it. The rights of a biological father supersede any contrary provisions in a will—as I'm sure you're aware."

Of course, he was aware—he just didn't appreciate the fact that she'd chosen his brother to be the legal guardian of his child. If he thought about it rationally, he knew that Kelly's long-standing friendship with Lukas made him a logical choice. But he wasn't thinking very rationally about anything right now.

"Your peas are thawed," he told her, and handed the bag across the table.

"I've got corn, too, if your jaw's still sore," she offered.

He moved it carefully from side to side. "No, it's good."

She got up to toss the package of peas into the sink.

"What are you and…Ava doing on Saturday?"

If she noticed the slight hesitation before he said her daughter's name, she ignored it. "Back-to-school shopping."

"All day?"

She smiled at that. "You've obviously never shopped with a twelve-year-old girl."

"Obviously," he agreed, and gave himself credit for

not shuddering at the very thought. "How about Saturday night?"

"Why?"

"Because I was thinking maybe we should spend some time together...." The suggestion trailed off when he saw that Kelly was already shaking her head. "Why not?"

"I just think it's too soon. Until you've actually accepted the truth, you're going to be looking for any tiny piece of evidence to support your hope that Ava's not your daughter."

He frowned and pushed away from the table to take his empty mug to the counter. "I don't know what I hope."

"Your instant and vehement denial when I told you about Ava proved, at least to me, that you don't want to be a father."

"Right now, I'm not sure what I want," he admitted.

But when he turned to face her, he realized that she was now trapped between the counter at her back and him at her front. He knew the smart thing would be to step away, but he didn't. Instead, he lifted his hand and brushed his thumb gently over the curve of her bottom lip.

Her breath hitched, her eyes darkened. "Jacks."

He didn't know if she'd spoken his name in warning or request, and he didn't care. Despite their complicated history, there was something about being in close proximity to Kelly that made him forget everything else and simply burn with need. Heat flared in his belly, pulsed through his veins. He might not *want* to want her, but there was no denying that he did.

"Actually, that's not entirely true," he told her. "I do know what I want—at least in some respects."

She put her hand on his chest and shook her head. "Don't do this, Jackson."

"Don't do what?" he challenged, his lips hovering only inches above hers.

"Kiss me."

He ignored the "don't" and, focusing on the "kiss me" part, brushed his lips against hers.

He wasn't the kind of man who gave in to impulse. At least not since that night he'd taken Kelly back to his hotel room more than thirteen years earlier. But being so close to her now, he found he didn't have the willpower to resist what he wanted. *Just one little taste,* he promised himself. Just a sample of her flavor, to prove to himself that she wasn't nearly as intoxicating as he recalled and rid himself of the haunting memories.

But that sample proved otherwise; one little taste wasn't nearly enough. He settled his mouth over hers, and slowly deepened the kiss. Her resistance melted like a double scoop of ice cream in the August sun—slowly and sweetly. And her flavor was even sweeter.

He traced the shape of her mouth with the tip of his tongue, felt her breath shudder out between her lips. The hand she'd laid against his chest was no longer trying to push him away but clutching at the fabric of his shirt.

He'd wanted to do this since he'd seen her at the airport. Not that he would have admitted it, even to himself, but he'd felt the flare of desire in that first moment when her gaze locked with his. And now that he had her in his arms, he wasn't even close to being ready to let her go.

Then the screen at the back door banged against its frame, and she froze.

"Mom?"

Jack was already stepping back before Kelly pushed him away.

"In the kitchen." She picked up a cloth and began to wipe down the already spotless counter.

Ava poked her head inside the doorway. "Can I hang out next door with the twins and the puppies for a while?"

"If it's okay with Mrs. Garrett."

The child rolled her eyes. "She's the one who told me to check with you."

"Then it's okay with me," Kelly allowed.

"Great." She was gone again as quickly as she'd entered, without ever noticing that Jack was standing on the other side of the room.

But he noticed that Kelly's hands weren't quite steady as she carefully folded the cloth and draped it over the faucet. Had she been as shaken as he by the kiss they'd shared? Or was she simply unnerved by the fact that her daughter had very nearly walked in on them together?

He might have initiated the kiss, but there was no doubt that Kelly had been an enthusiastic participant, and he couldn't help but speculate about how far things might have gone if Ava hadn't interrupted. But maybe he didn't want to know. He suspected that the memory of that kiss was going to be more than enough to keep him awake at night without imagining how Kelly's skin would have felt beneath his fingertips, how her body would have responded to his touch.

He forced those thoughts aside to ask, "Does Ava spend a lot of time with Shane and Quinn?"

Kelly took a deep frying pan out of the cupboard and set it on top of the stove. "She likes to play big sister, and the twins don't seem to mind her bossing them around."

"They might not be siblings, but they could be her cousins—by marriage, if not by blood."

She nodded, confirming that she'd already considered the possibility. When she'd told him that Ava was his child, he'd only thought about how that revelation affected him.

He hadn't considered that his daughter would be a niece to each of his brothers.

Obviously the situation was a lot more complicated than he'd realized—and that was before he'd kissed Kelly.

On Saturday, Kelly took Ava shopping. She wanted to make sure that her daughter had everything she needed to start the new school year and, even more importantly, she wanted to spend some time with her. Ava still wasn't happy about the move, and although she kept in frequent contact with Rachel and some of her other friends online, she was feeling a little lonely.

Kelly knew from personal experience that it wasn't easy to move to a new town and start over again. She'd been a couple of years younger than Ava when she'd been dumped at her grandmother's house in Pinehurst because her father was a long-distance trucker who was gone more than he was home and her mother couldn't handle full-time care of a child on her own. What was originally supposed to be a few weeks had somehow turned into months, and then into years. On her first day of school, she'd been absolutely terrified. And it hadn't been so long ago that she couldn't remember the tangle of knots in her stomach that had made her want to throw up the cereal she'd had for breakfast.

She'd stopped at the corner and stared at the crowd of students already milling around outside of Parkdale Elementary School. Other kids moved past her, most of them in groups, talking and laughing, their friendships established over the years that they'd been together. She didn't know how long she stood there, trying to ignore the churning in her stomach and summon the courage to move forward, when she saw Jackson and Lukas coming toward her.

The Garrett brothers lived next door to her grandmother, so she'd gotten to know them a little bit over the summer.

Lukas was her age, Jackson was three years older, and Matthew was two years older than him and in high school already. But she didn't know much more than that, and she was more than a little surprised when Lukas stopped beside her. Jackson scowled and mumbled something under his breath, but Lukas just waved him on.

"Trying to decide whether to go forward or back?" Lukas asked.

Though her cheeks had flushed with embarrassment that he'd been able to read her thoughts so easily, she nodded.

"If we had Mrs. Vanderheide, I'd tell you to go back. I'd even go with you," he said. "But Miss Ellis isn't too bad."

It was all he said, but he stood patiently, waiting until she was ready. And when she was confident that the Frosted Flakes were going to stay in her stomach, she turned toward the school and he fell into step beside her.

She'd lucked out that day, and she was keeping her fingers crossed that Ava might be half as lucky with the friends she made at her new school—or maybe even before then. Though her daughter wasn't looking forward to camp ("summer camp is for babies"), Kelly was hopeful that she would meet some kids there who would be in her class at Parkdale when school started up in a few weeks.

But for now, mother and daughter were focused on shopping. Of course, Ava complained that all of the stores at the mall and even the more upscale shops in the village were completely lame. Despite that fact, however, she managed to find a couple of pairs of jeans, a skirt, several T-shirts, three sweaters, various accessories and a new backpack. The only real dissension occurred when they passed Gia's Salon & Spa and Ava decided that she wanted more streaks put in her hair. Kelly nixed that plan but suggested that, after several hours of shopping, they both deserved to pamper their feet.

By the time they left the spa, it was almost seven o'clock. Since they were already out and just down the street from Mama Leone's, Kelly decided to treat her daughter to dinner out.

As they made their way to the restaurant, Kelly realized she was smiling. It had been a good day, with only a few minor bumps along the way, and she was thrilled that she'd had the time to reconnect with her daughter.

Her smile slipped when the hostess led them to the back of the restaurant and they passed the table where Jackson was seated across from a beautiful blonde with glossy red lips and fingernails to match the spandex dress that emphasized her impressive curves. His gaze never wavered from his companion, for which Kelly was grateful. She didn't want him to know that she was there, and she wasn't thrilled about the possibility that Ava might spot him, either.

So she made sure that Ava was seated with her back to them, which meant that Kelly was facing their table. And while Jackson flirted with his date, she couldn't help but remember that he'd been kissing her less than twenty-four hours earlier.

It was one kiss, but that one kiss had unleashed a tidal wave of memories that kept her tossing and turning through the night. It wasn't fair that he should still be able to affect her. It wasn't fair that he could kiss her like he'd kissed her yesterday and move on to seducing another woman tonight.

But that was Jackson. She'd known his reputation all those years before, but she'd chosen to overlook it. She'd believed—in her youthful naïveté—that once he was with her, he would realize he loved her as much as she loved him. He would forget that he'd ever wanted anyone else, and they would be together forever.

Obviously things hadn't gone according to her plan. For

Kelly, the weekend they spent together in Chicago only cemented her feelings. For Jackson, it was merely a brief interlude in his life—she was merely one of numerous women who had shared his bed.

And here he was again now, with another woman, proving to Kelly that he hadn't changed at all. He was still a player. And so what? That one kiss aside, she had no intention of resuming any kind of relationship with him. His personal life wasn't any of her business, but she did worry about Ava and how she might respond to the parade of women through her father's life.

Right now, though, she was going to put Jackson out of her mind and focus on her daughter. She *wasn't* going to watch Miss Scarlet feed him bites of her cheesecake. She *didn't* care that the blonde then put the fork to her own lips and slowly licked the tines, obviously savoring his flavor even more than the dessert. Instead, Kelly dropped her gaze and stabbed her own fork into a wedge of tomato.

Ava had already finished her salad and dug into her seven-cheese ravioli with enthusiasm. Kelly forced down a few more bites of lettuce and wondered again if she'd made a mistake in coming back to Pinehurst.

She'd been certain that he would have changed in the past thirteen years. But seeing him here tonight, she realized that was her mistake. He wasn't the man she wanted him to be, and the fact that she was disappointed by that realization was her fault more than his. She hadn't been hoping for any kind of reconciliation with Jackson when she decided to come back—but she had hoped that he could be the father her daughter deserved. Now she knew otherwise.

He finished his coffee and signed the check. Then he offered his hand to the blonde, and she stood up, tottering a little on her skyscraper heels. And when she smiled at him, the curve of her lushly painted lips was full of promise.

Jackson momentarily shifted his attention away from his date—and his gaze collided with hers. She saw the range of emotions cross over his face: recognition, surprise, guilt. It was Kelly who broke the connection, deliberately looking away to prove that she didn't care, that his presence didn't matter, that *he* didn't matter.

But as she poked at her angel hair pasta, she knew it was a lie. The truth was, he'd always mattered to her. Too much.

"Mom—is something wrong?"

Kelly glanced up, forced a smile. "Of course not."

Ava gestured to her plate. "You said you were starving, but you haven't even touched your meal."

"I guess I wasn't as hungry as I thought."

"I'm still hungry," Ava told her.

"Did you want some of my pasta?"

Her daughter shook her head. "Can I have dessert?" she asked hopefully.

Kelly was grateful to realize that some things in life were still simple, and her smile came more easily this time. "You can absolutely have dessert."

"Can we get it to go? There's a movie on TV tonight that I thought we could watch."

Her daughter was actually initiating a plan to spend more time with her? Kelly couldn't have been more pleased. "Sounds good to me."

When they got home, they put their pajamas on and snuggled on the couch together. While Ava watched her movie, Kelly's thoughts wandered. Nothing had gone as she'd planned so far. She hadn't expected Jackson to immediately embrace the fact of fatherhood, but she hadn't anticipated an outright rejection of the claim, either. And while he seemed to be coming around to accepting the truth, Lukas wasn't even talking to her.

She had no intention of going back to Seattle. All of

the reasons she had for leaving were still valid. But maybe she should have considered moving somewhere other than Pinehurst, somewhere where she wouldn't be haunted by memories of the hopes and dreams she'd had so long ago. Except that no other place had ever felt like home. Pinehurst was where she wanted to raise her daughter, and she was confident that Ava would make friends quickly and be happy here.

She didn't realize the movie had finished until she saw the credits rolling on the screen. Pushing her questions and uncertainties aside, she nudged her sleepy daughter up the stairs and tucked her into bed.

"Mom?"

"Hmm?"

"Thanks for today. It was kind of fun—hanging out with you."

And with those words, the last of Kelly's reservations was obliterated. Because she knew now that, regardless of what happened with Jackson, she had done the right thing by bringing Ava to Pinehurst. She brushed the hair away from her daughter's face and touched her lips to her forehead. "Me, too."

She and her daughter had each other and that was enough—neither of them needed Jackson Garrett.

Unfortunately, that didn't stop Kelly from wanting him.

Chapter Five

It was a sign of how complicated his life had gotten in the space of a single week that Jack left a willing woman on her doorstep Saturday night and went home to his empty bed to dream about another.

He woke up alone, aroused, and cursing Kelly Cooper.

She'd turned his entire life upside down with the proclamation that he was the father of her child. Actually, she'd turned his entire life upside down simply by walking back into it. Because even after thirteen years, she was the one woman he'd never been able to forget.

If he'd been a romantic, he might have thought she was "the one who got away"—except that he'd purposefully sent her away because he'd believed it was the right thing to do. When she'd been a kid hanging out with his younger brother, he'd sometimes caught her looking at him with something like hero worship in her eyes. He'd been flattered and amused by her attention, but when he'd gone off to college, he hadn't thought too much about her harmless infatuation or her.

And then he'd come home for Christmas that first year to discover that Kelly Cooper wasn't a kid anymore. Somehow in the four months that he'd been gone, she'd grown up. The skinny kid with a mouthful of braces had become a stunning beauty with interesting curves in all the right places. And suddenly that infatuation wasn't quite so harmless anymore, not when he was experiencing feelings he shouldn't be experiencing for his little brother's best friend.

But he'd kept his wayward emotions in check, at least until her birthday the following summer.

Shirley Lawson had hosted a sweet sixteen party for her granddaughter in the backyard, complete with bouquets of pink and white balloons, miles of streamers fluttering in the breeze and a multi-tiered birthday cake. Jack hadn't planned on stopping in at the party. He had other plans for the evening already in place—and he was confident that the evening would end with Leesa Webster in the backseat of his Mustang up at Eagle Point Park.

He was on his way to the car when he glanced over and noticed that Kelly was standing alone on the front porch while music and laughter sounded from the back of the house. He tucked his keys in his pocket and walked over to her.

"Isn't the birthday girl supposed to be at the birthday party?"

She smiled. "I just wanted to take a break from the crowd for a minute."

"It is quite a crowd," he noted, climbing the steps toward her.

"Sweet sixteen is a milestone, according to Grandma."

"Sixteen I believe," he teased. "But sweet?"

She responded with a sassy smile. "I am sweet," she assured him. "But I'm not as innocent as you think."

It was a challenge—and one he couldn't resist any longer. He tipped her chin up. "Let's see about that," he said, and brushed his lips over hers.

Her golden eyes widened momentarily, then drifted shut. Her mouth was soft—softer than he'd anticipated, moist and sweetly yielding. She lifted her arms to link them behind his neck as her body melted against his.

He touched his tongue to the seam of her lips, a question more than a demand, and she answered by opening for him. Her tongue touched his, tentatively at first, then more boldly. She had some experience with kissing, or she was a fast learner, but he would bet the Mustang he'd recently emptied his bank account to buy that she hadn't done much more than that.

The realization should have succeeded in lessening his desire; instead, her innocence had the opposite effect. He wanted to touch where no one else had touched, make her feel things no one else had made her feel. But for now, he contented himself with kissing her, savoring the flavor of her lips and the softness of her curves pressed against him.

She was sweet...and, his conscience belatedly reminded him, only sixteen.

He eased his lips from hers.

Kelly looked up at him, her eyes dark and silently questioning.

"You're still too innocent for me," he said with genuine regret.

She blew out a slow, shaky breath as he took a step back.

"You're not staying for cake?"

He shook his head. "I have to go."

She shrugged, as if she didn't care, but he could see that she was hurt and confused—and more than willing to finish what they'd started. And as much as he'd been looking forward to his date with Leesa, he knew he wouldn't take her up to Eagle Point Park tonight. He couldn't be with her when he'd be thinking about Kelly.

But before he walked away, he brushed his thumb gently over her bottom lip, which was erotically swollen from his kiss. "Happy Birthday, Kelly."

That had been the beginning of the end for Jack. From

that moment, all of his best intentions had gone straight to hell.

He hadn't made another move that summer—he hadn't dared. Because he'd known that if he put his hands on Kelly again, she wouldn't stop him, and he hadn't trusted that he'd be able to stop himself.

And then Kelly had left Pinehurst before the ink was even dry on her high school diploma, heading off to college in Chicago. She'd come back for the summer after her first year, intending to take care of her grandmother while she recovered from a stroke. But a second blood clot interrupted those plans, and after the funeral, Kelly had gone back to Chicago again.

It was two years after that before Jack saw her again, before they spent those three glorious days and nights together.

Three glorious days and nights that had resulted in Kelly having his child.

No wonder she wasn't infatuated with him anymore. In fact, if he had to guess, he would say that whatever she felt for him now was closer to the opposite end of the emotional spectrum. She might not like him, but she wanted him. It wasn't arrogance or delusion that made him think so, but a simple assessment of her physical response to his nearness.

She didn't want to want him, but the chemistry was undeniable. And when he'd kissed her, she'd definitely kissed him back, confirming that she wasn't nearly as disinterested as she wanted him to believe.

It was his frustration with Kelly that had made him amenable to Norah Hennessey Sinclair's invitation to dinner the night before. Frustration combined with determination to not sit at home and think about her—or his still-convoluted feelings about her daughter. *His daughter.*

Those two words still made him break out in a cold

sweat, and although his thoughts had finally shifted from denial to acceptance, he didn't know what would come next. Dinner with a client had offered a welcome reprieve from his own thoughts. He certainly hadn't given Norah any indication he was interested in sharing anything more than a meal.

He'd been more annoyed than enticed by her drunken and obvious attempt at seduction. Even if she hadn't been inebriated, he wouldn't have been tempted. As a client, she was strictly off-limits, and even aside from that, he didn't do casual hook-ups anymore. Hadn't in a long time. But mostly it was because, while Norah's foot had been climbing inside his pant leg under the table, he hadn't been able to stop thinking about Kelly.

Then he'd looked up, and his gaze had locked with hers. And the look in her eyes, the cool contempt in her golden gaze, told him more clearly than any words how she'd interpreted the scene. Although it irked him that he even cared what she thought, he couldn't deny that he did.

Kelly had planned to spend most of the day Sunday reviewing the information Craig Richmond had sent to her about Richmond Pharmaceuticals. Then she woke up to find the sun spilling into her bedroom and decided the review could wait until after the sun went down. It was too nice a day to be stuck indoors and there were gardens to be tended.

She'd tried to persuade Ava to come outside with her, but her daughter had decided to weed through her closet instead. She was sorting through her clothes and discarding those that she didn't want anymore. Kelly had suggested that she do exactly that before they packed everything up in Seattle and shipped it halfway across the country, but of course Ava had resisted.

Kelly didn't mind working alone, and she found the outdoor chores surprisingly relaxing. Her twelfth-floor condo in Seattle hadn't boasted any kind of yard, but she'd had a balcony. Every spring, she'd filled it with baskets and pots of flowers.

As it turned out, she wasn't alone for very long. Quinn and Shane and Finnigan and Frederick—the adorable twins from next door and their energetic puppies—ventured over to see what she was doing, and so that Finn could "water" the alyssum. And then, a short while after that, Mrs. Dunford wandered across the street to see how Kelly and Ava were settling in.

She didn't mind the interruptions. In fact, casual drop-ins and easy conversations with neighbors were some of the reasons Kelly was glad to be back in Pinehurst. Or so she thought until Jackson stopped by.

He parked in front of the house and casually strolled up the walk. He was wearing a blue golf shirt that stretched across the breadth of his shoulders and a pair of well-worn jeans that molded to the strong muscles of his thighs, and with each step that drew him nearer, her heart started to pound just a little bit faster.

"I wouldn't have guessed that you had a green thumb," he mused.

"I'm not sure that I do," she responded in a similarly casual tone. "But I like flowers."

He hooked his thumbs into the front pockets of his jeans and gave her a leisurely once-over. "You should have a hat on—your nose is looking a little red."

She rubbed the back of her hand over it, shrugged. "Is that why you're here, Jackson—as a representative of the SPF police?"

His lips curved, just a little. "No, I actually came to see my brother."

"He lives over there," she reminded him, pointing to the house next door.

"*And* I was hoping to see you."

"Why?"

"I wanted to explain."

Kelly didn't ask what he was talking about. In that brief moment of eye contact at the restaurant, too much had passed between them for her to pretend otherwise. Instead, she only said, "No explanation necessary."

"I know what you're thinking."

She hacked at the roots of a stubborn weed with her trowel. "Do you?"

"Yeah. And before you try and execute me, you should know that the woman I was with at the restaurant last night is a client."

She almost laughed out loud. If he was going to insist on offering an explanation, she would have expected something a little more creative than that. Or at least more credible.

And though she didn't want to ask—because asking would suggest that she cared, and she didn't want to care—the words spilled out, anyway, and with enough of an edge to belie the casual disinterest she wanted to project. "Do you usually conduct business with wine and candlelight?"

"No." He took off his sunglasses and tucked them into the pocket of his golf shirt. "But it's not unusual to meet a client outside of the office, so when she called and suggested a meeting at Mama Leone's, I didn't see any reason not to agree."

Kelly hacked at another weed, probably more viciously than was necessary.

"I handled her divorce a few years back," he continued. "She's thinking about getting married again and wanted to talk about a prenup."

"Yeah, she looked like a woman who was in a committed relationship with someone else," she noted dryly.

"She was at the restaurant before me and already halfway through the bottle of wine when I got there. I had one glass, she finished off the rest with her dinner, then I drove her home."

"She was feeding you off of her fork."

"She asked if I wanted to try the cheesecake, I said no thanks. She held the fork out to me, and when I tried to decline again, she stabbed me in the mouth with the tines. I figured sampling the cake was a better alternative than a bloody lip."

Kelly remained skeptical. From her perspective, she hadn't seen any evidence of Jack resisting the woman's advances. But if the woman truly was exploiting their professional relationship to put the moves on him, she could see how that would have put him in an awkward situation. Or maybe she was an idiot for wanting to believe any part of his explanation.

"And the reason she was plastered to your side as you left the restaurant?" She shook her head and held up a hand before he could answer. "You know what? It doesn't matter. It's really not any of my business."

"I think I have some pretty good reasons to be angry with you—but why are you mad at me?"

"I'm not mad at you."

"You sound mad," he noted.

She huffed out a breath. "If I'm mad, it's at myself."

His brows rose. "Care to explain that one?"

"I was...surprised to see you with her," she admitted. "And then I realized I shouldn't have been."

"I'm still not sure I understand."

"I thought you'd changed. I'd *hoped* you'd changed."

She stood up and brushed her hands down the front of her shorts. "That was my mistake."

His gaze narrowed. "You think I was kissing you in your kitchen one day and seducing another woman the next?"

She didn't bother to deny it.

"Dammit, Kelly, I didn't sleep with her."

"I don't care who you sleep with," she finally told him. "But I would appreciate it if you exercised a little discretion—for Ava's sake, if no one else's."

She picked up the basket of gardening tools and started to turn away, but he caught her arm, halting her escape. She didn't try to pull away; she knew he wouldn't release her until he was ready. Instead, she looked at him with what she hoped was casual disinterest.

"I didn't sleep with her," he said again, the icy tone of his voice a stark contrast to the heated fury in his eyes. "And when I do take a woman to my bed, I prefer that her faculties aren't impaired by alcohol."

"Too much of a gentleman to take advantage of an intoxicated female?"

"No," he corrected her. "Too demanding to settle for any less than equal and eager participation." His hand trailed down her arm, slid behind her back to draw her closer. "As I remember it, you were definitely an equal, and very eager, participant."

"That was a long time ago," she reminded him.

"I'm looking forward to having you in my bed again."

It wasn't arrogance in his tone, but confidence, and his absolute certainty made everything inside her tremble. But there was no way she was going to let him see it. She wasn't an infatuated twenty-one-year-old anymore, and she tilted her head back to meet the challenge in his gaze head-on.

"When I take a man to *my* bed, I prefer if he's not inhibited by his ego."

Jackson's lips curved in a slow and devastatingly sexy smile. "Then we understand one another."

But as Kelly watched him cross the grass toward the house next door, she realized that she didn't understand anything, least of all the tangle of emotions inside of her.

After Jackson had gone over to his brother's house, Kelly moved around to the backyard and continued with her gardening as if the encounter had never happened. Thankfully there was no one around to witness her distraction when she yanked a petunia out of the dirt.

What was wrong with her that she could still get tangled up in knots over the man who had broken her heart thirteen years earlier? She'd been so sure that she was over him, that the only connection between them was their daughter. But when he looked at her, when his eyes skimmed over her from head to toe in slow and blatantly masculine perusal, every hormone in her body went on full alert. It was a complication she hadn't been prepared for and definitely didn't need.

Since her divorce almost a decade earlier, she could count on one hand the number of sexual liaisons she'd had—with two fingers left over. And she honestly hadn't felt as if she was missing out on anything.

As far as she was concerned, the whole dating and mating thing was hugely overrated. Especially when most of her time and energy was focused on raising her daughter and building a career. So why was it, after only five minutes with Jackson Garrett, she couldn't think about anything else but him?

"Am I interrupting?"

Kelly glanced up at Georgia. "Yes," she said. "And thank you."

Her neighbor chuckled. "Are the weeds winning the battle?"

"No—it's not the garden but my own wandering thoughts." She dropped her gloves and trowel on top of the basket she'd filled with weeds—and one broken purple petunia. "I just finished."

"The boys and I baked too many cookies." She gestured with the plate she carried. "So I was hoping I could pawn some off on you and Ava."

"Anytime you want to pawn cookies, we're more than happy to help." Kelly headed back toward the house. "I put a pot of coffee on before I came out, if you want a cup."

"Maybe half a cup," Georgia allowed. "I'm still nursing."

Kelly smiled. "I remember those days—and how much I missed my daily jolt of java."

Georgia followed her into the kitchen, set the plate of cookies on the table. "I almost manage to convince myself that I don't miss it, and then I'll walk past the Bean There Café and catch the scent of freshly roasted beans in the air, and I actually get weak in the knees."

"I know what you mean." Kelly took two mugs out of the cupboard, poured half a cup in one for Georgia. "Milk?"

The other woman shook her head. "Matt thinks Pippa is lactose intolerant. She went through a really bad colicky phase that finally eased when I cut milk from my diet."

"I've heard horror stories about colic," Kelly admitted, filling her own cup to the top. "Thankfully, I didn't have to deal with that with Ava."

"The twins were good, too," Georgia told her. "It was just hard because there were two of them. And maybe my memory of those early days has faded, but I know I wasn't nearly as sleep-deprived caring for the two of them as I was in the first few months with Pippa. Of course, I wasn't on my own when Quinn and Shane were babies, either."

"I had a wonderful neighbor who was happy to pitch in whenever I was ready to pull my hair out, and I never felt like I was on my own when she was around." Kelly picked up a cookie and smiled. "Bev liked to bake, too." Then she bit into the treat, and sighed with pleasure. "Oh, these are heaven."

"Chocolate chip are Matt's favorite, and the boys wanted to help make them this time. The plan was for them to take turns measuring out ingredients—instead they each measured everything, so we doubled the batch."

"They should help you bake more often," Kelly suggested.

Georgia smiled. "There's some peanut butter, too, because they're Jack's favorite. Quinn and Shane wanted to thank him for taking them to see *Ted E. Bear's Birthday*."

Kelly paused with a cookie halfway toward her mouth. "Jackson took your boys to see a kids' movie?"

"Matt was supposed to take them when I went to Megan Richmond's baby shower, but he got called into the hospital, so Jack stepped in."

"Was there bribery or blackmail involved?"

Her neighbor chuckled. "Not that I'm aware of."

"Because the Jackson Garrett I used to know would have run far and fast in the opposite direction of a movie theater full of preschoolers."

"A few months ago, he probably would have," Georgia agreed. "And while I was a little concerned about his reputation in the beginning, I have to admit, I've developed something of a soft spot for Jack."

"Now you've piqued my curiosity," Kelly admitted.

"When I first moved in, even before Matt and I were officially dating, Jack warned me off."

"I can see how that would endear him to you," she said dryly.

Georgia laughed. "What it showed me is that, despite his casual and cavalier attitude, he is close to his family, cares deeply about people and has protective instincts."

Kelly was skeptical, but since she'd been gone for a lot of years, she really couldn't disagree with any part of that assessment. So all she said was, "Even as kids, they were close. The three brothers would—and often did— fight with one another, but against anyone else, they always stuck together."

"They still stick together," Georgia said. "Usually on Sunday afternoons in front of the television, watching whatever sport is in season."

"Is Lukas there today?" Kelly asked, keeping her tone deliberately casual.

The other woman shook her head. "No. He called earlier to say that he was behind on his paperwork at the clinic."

Kelly would have bet that Lukas wanted to avoid another confrontation with Jackson more than he wanted to catch up on paperwork. And she knew that was her fault, but she didn't have the first clue how to fix it.

The clatter of footsteps on the stairs drew her attention back to the present.

"Hey, Mom, can we go— Oh, hi, Mrs. Garrett."

"Hello, Ava."

"Where did you want to go?" Kelly asked her.

"Back to that store at the mall, the one where I got the green top." She smiled coaxingly. "I think they had it in purple, too."

"Maybe tomorrow."

Ava sighed, obviously disappointed. Then her gaze landed on the plate in the middle of the table and her eyes lit up. "Cookies?"

Georgia laughed. "Help yourself."

Ava zeroed straight in on the peanut butter, forcing Kelly to acknowledge that the truth about her daughter's paternity couldn't remain a secret forever.

Chapter Six

By Wednesday night, Jack had spent more than enough time alone with his thoughts and still didn't have any answers to the questions that plagued his mind. He needed to talk to someone. He didn't necessarily want advice so much as he wanted to vent. And since there was no one outside his immediate family who he would trust with the information, his choices were limited.

He didn't even consider going to see Lukas. His younger brother had made his feelings about the situation more than clear when he'd introduced his fist to Jack's face the week before. Though the bruise on his jaw had already faded, Jack wasn't willing to chance a repeat performance. Which is why he found himself dialing Matt's number.

Less than thirty minutes later, his brother was at the door.

"I'm sorry to drag you away from your wife and kids," Jack apologized.

Matt took the bottle of Millhouse his brother opened for him. "The offer of beer and a baseball game aside, I know you wouldn't have asked me to come over if it wasn't important."

Jack nodded. "It's about Kelly."

Matt paused with his bottle halfway to his lips. "Kelly? Or Ava?"

He scowled as he dropped onto the opposite end of the couch. "She told you?"

"She didn't tell me anything," Matt said.

"Then it was Lukas," he guessed.

"No one told me—no one had to," his brother assured him. "The first time I saw Kelly's daughter, I figured she had to be yours."

Jack hadn't been prepared for his brother's simple and ready acceptance—especially when it contradicted his continued denials. "You really think so?"

Matt shook his head. "I can't believe *you* doubt it. There's no mistaking the fact that Ava's a Garrett, even if it doesn't say so on her birth certificate. And since I know neither Luke nor I ever slept with Kelly, that narrows the choice of paternal prospects down considerably."

He tipped his bottle to his lips, giving himself a moment to consider his brother's logic. "Luke is furious with me."

"I'd bet he's even more furious with Kelly right now," Matt told him. "From the beginning, Ava has called him 'Uncle Lukas,' but he never knew that he really was her uncle."

"She never told me that she was pregnant," Jack told him.

"And if she had told you—what would you have done?"

Damn, his brother always asked the tough questions. It was the same one Jack had been asking himself since Kelly had dropped her bombshell in his office. And it was a question to which he still didn't have an answer. "I was engaged to Sara," he reminded Matt.

His brother frowned. "While you were sleeping with Kelly?"

"No. Of course not." His reputation aside, Jack had never been one to juggle women. He might not stick with anyone for very long, but he wasn't a cheater. "What happened with Kelly—it was one weekend, after Sara had given me back her ring."

"I don't need the details," Matt told him.

Jack took a long swallow from his bottle. "I don't know anything about being a father."

"No one does in the beginning, but you'll learn."

Jack wasn't so sure that he would—or even that he wanted to. Almost a week after Kelly's visit to his office, his head was still spinning, and whenever he let himself think *I'm a father,* his heart would start to race with as much apprehension as anticipation. "I had everything I wanted—a successful career, an executive condo, female companionship when I wanted it, and peace and quiet when I didn't."

"And now you have a child to add to the mix."

"Yeah." And Jack suspected it was going to be like trying to mix oil and water.

"She's a great kid," Matt noted.

It was, he knew, the same sentiment Lukas had frequently expressed, and it frustrated him that both of his brothers could speak with such authority about the child with whom he'd barely exchanged half a dozen words. "I wouldn't know."

"So get to know her," his brother suggested, unfazed by the irritation in Jack's voice.

"Do you really think it's going to be that easy?"

"I don't think it's going to be easy at all," Matt acknowledged. "But nothing worthwhile usually is."

He was probably right. The bigger problem was that Jack didn't have the first clue about how to relate to a twelve-year-old girl. Thankfully, he still had some time to figure things out. "Cam said the DNA results would take about ten days."

Matt frowned. "Do you really need some lab report to confirm what you already know?"

"But I don't know," Jack told him.

"Stop being a lawyer for five minutes and tell me what you feel in your gut."

Jack scowled. "What's wrong with wanting proof?"

Matt sat back and studied his brother across the table. "You're not in denial because you don't want it to be true," he realized. "You're hesitant to take the next step because you *do* want it to be true and you're afraid that it might not be."

"Maybe you should have been the lawyer, because that's the kind of convoluted reasoning I usually hear in the courthouse."

His brother ignored the snide comment. "It was more than a fling, wasn't it?" he asked instead.

"What?"

"You and Kelly," Matt clarified. "You never got over her, did you?"

"We spent one weekend together more than a dozen years ago—there wasn't much to get over," Jack assured him.

"And yet…" his brother mused thoughtfully.

"And yet *nothing*."

"So why haven't you ever fallen in love?"

"That's an odd question from the brother who was the best man at my wedding," Jack noted.

"Did you love Sara?" Matt asked him now. "Or were you trying to forget about Kelly when you got back together with her?"

It occurred to Jack that maybe he should have called Lukas, because the impact of his younger brother's fist was less uncomfortable than his older brother's speculation. Unwilling to answer Matt's question, he picked up the remote and turned on the ball game. And breathed a sigh of relief when his brother didn't press him for a response.

He wasn't prepared to admit that he'd reconciled with

Sara not because he wanted to forget about Kelly but because he knew he had to. Because Lukas had called him, seeking advice after Kelly had confessed to her best friend that she'd fallen in love and was thinking about leaving school. And he was tired of being the bad guy for doing the right thing.

Except that, now that he knew about Ava, he wasn't sure it had been the right thing, after all.

Kelly didn't like feeling off-balance, but she hadn't felt steady or sure about anything since she'd stepped off the airplane and seen Jackson at the airport. And he, predictably, enjoyed flustering her. From the mind-numbing kiss in her kitchen to his arrogant assertion that he would have her in his bed again, he continually used the sexual tension between them to undermine her control. But she was determined to take it back.

She decided that the best way to do that was to make the next move—to act instead of react—and to keep the focus of the conversation on Ava. So when she stopped in the village after a meeting at Richmond Pharmaceuticals Tuesday afternoon, she took out her cell phone and dialed the number of Jackson's office.

This time, he took her call.

"I'm just down the street from your office and thought I'd see if you had time for coffee."

"If you're at the Bean There Café, I can make time," he told her.

And he did, arriving at the café just as Kelly was carrying their beverages to a table. She sat down with her decadent caramel macchiato and passed him the oversize mug of dark roast. "I wanted to invite you to come over for dinner Friday night."

His lips curved as he lifted the mug, just enough to

make her heart pound a little bit faster and throw her off-balance again.

"Are you asking me on a date?"

She huffed out a breath. "No, I'm asking if you want to share a meal with me *and Ava*."

He sipped his coffee. "You're no longer concerned that I'll be looking for any tiny bit of evidence that she's not mine?"

"I'm not concerned that you'll find any," she said evenly. "So are you interested?"

His gaze dropped to her mouth, lingered. "Oh, I think you know I'm interested."

Less than two minutes in his company, and she'd already lost control of the conversation—and her hormones. She wrapped her hands around the mug and tried to get a grip on her wayward thoughts. "How do you do that?"

"Do what?"

"Turn everything into innuendo."

"It's a gift," he said mildly.

She shook her head. "I thought you hated me."

"I don't have to like you to want you."

She lifted a brow. "Do you usually have sex with women you don't like?"

"No—liking is usually a minimal requirement," he told her. "But nothing between us has ever been usual."

She couldn't deny that was true. "Getting back to my question—are you interested in coming for dinner? Or do you have other plans?"

"What are you making?"

"Really? That's going to be the deciding factor for you?"

"No, I was just wondering," he said. "I'm definitely interested in dinner and I don't have other plans. But won't Ava think it's strange that I'm coming for dinner? Or do you frequently cook for male guests?"

"Are you asking about my social life?"

"One more thing I'm curious about."

"Well, I can assure you that mine isn't nearly as busy or varied as yours."

"You shouldn't believe everything you hear," he warned.

"Dinner?" she prompted, refusing to be sidetracked again.

"What time?"

"Six thirty."

He nodded and picked up his mug. "That works for me."

Kelly sipped her macchiato.

"Have you told Ava anything about me?" Jackson asked.

"Do you mean specifically about you—or generally about her father?"

"About her father," he clarified.

"Not really," she admitted. "I've never lied to her, but I haven't volunteered much information, either. She went through a phase where she asked a lot of questions, but I managed to deflect most of them, and I think she got used to it just being the two of us."

"That's going to change," he said.

It wasn't a threat or a warning, just a simple statement of fact, and she nodded. She *wanted* it to change. She wanted Ava to know her father, as she'd never known her own. But somehow it had been easier to want those things for her daughter when they were living three thousand miles away and there was little chance of actually getting them. Now that she was sitting across the table from Ava's father, she couldn't help but worry that she'd started on a journey that might not end where she wanted.

"I want to tell her that I'm her father," he said, when she remained silent.

And once again, he'd thrown her for a loop. His statement didn't just surprise her, it left her completely baffled by the change in his attitude.

"I thought you were still in denial about that."

He shook his head. "I've missed more than twelve years of her life already, and I don't want to wait another week for the test results to tell Ava."

"Suddenly you believe that I'm telling the truth? That I didn't give birth to someone else's baby for the sole purpose of hitting you up for child support a dozen years later?"

He winced. "I hope it didn't sound that ridiculous when I suggested it."

"Not just ridiculous but insulting."

"Would it help if I said I was sorry?"

She looked at him over the rim of her cup. "Are you?"

"Yes." His response was immediate and sincere. "You caught me off-guard and it was a totally knee-jerk response."

"Well, the 'jerk' part sounds about right," she said.

"I am sorry," he said. "And I do want to know…my daughter."

The pause before "my daughter" was almost imperceptible, but she suspected that his hesitation this time wasn't because he didn't believe that she was "his" child but because he didn't know how to be her father.

Jackson Garrett—a man who could charm the most contrary female with little effort, who could face off against the most ornery judge without blinking an eye—was worried about impressing a twelve-year-old girl. And this brief glimpse of uncertainty from a man who was usually so overwhelmingly confident touched something deep in Kelly's heart.

"Let's start with dinner," she suggested.

Kelly treated her daughter to a movie Thursday night, hoping that while they watched the previews for coming attractions and munched on popcorn, she might have a chance to casually mention that Jackson would be coming over for dinner the following night. But the opportunity never seemed to arise—or maybe she was just reluctant to say anything that might affect the easy camaraderie they'd recently established.

On their way back home afterward, Kelly found herself driving by Lukas's house. He still lived on Terrace Avenue, in the redbrick back-split where he and his brothers had grown up. While Matt and Jack had each chosen to move out as soon they could afford to, Lukas had never seen any reason to move out of a home that so perfectly met all of his needs. Especially when one of those needs was adequate space for various creatures with fur, feathers or fins that he might be caring for at any given time. When Kelly saw the lights were on, she impulsively pulled into the driveway.

After the confrontation between Lukas and Jackson, she'd thought it was best to give him some time. And she'd been certain that, after a few days, Lukas would contact her. Except that six days had passed and she hadn't heard a single word. He had neither initiated any contact nor returned any of her calls. She knew he was probably still angry and upset, and that he had reason to be, but she wasn't going to let him continue to ignore her.

Ava didn't object to the detour. She'd always adored her uncle Lukas. And though she didn't know Matthew very well, she'd been spending a lot of time with Georgia and the kids, so she felt comfortable around their home and with the family. But there had been an uncharacteristic coolness when she'd met Jackson, and that worried Kelly. She didn't know if Ava sensed that Jackson wasn't at ease around her, or if she simply didn't like him. The latter would certainly make the father-daughter revelation even more awkward. Thankfully, that wasn't something Kelly needed to worry about just yet.

A cacophony of excited yips immediately sounded in response to the peal of the bell, and Ava's face lit up in anticipation of meeting the relation of Quinn and Shane's puppies. When Lukas opened the door, he had the wriggling animal tucked in the crook of his arm and icy reserve in his eyes. But the ice melted as soon as he saw Ava standing beside her mother.

He stepped back so that they could enter, and Ava immediately reached for the puppy. Einstein was thrilled by her attention and showed his enthusiasm by licking her whole face. Daphne, on the other hand, was a spoiled feline who had never been particularly fond of visitors invading her domain, and she stalked off to the upper floor to sulk when her master invited Kelly and Ava into the house.

"Did you want me to put on a pot of coffee—or are you in a hurry to get home?"

The tone of his question suggested to Kelly that he would prefer if she declined the less-than-gracious offer. But she had no intention of going anywhere until they'd reopened the lines of communication. "I'd love a cup of coffee."

Lukas's scowl deepened as he filled the reservoir with water and measured out the grounds. Thankfully, Ava seemed oblivious to his dark mood, and she babbled happily about the movie they'd just seen while she wrestled on the floor with the puppy.

When Lukas was finally pouring the coffee, Einstein headed toward the back door.

"Can I take him outside?" Ava asked Lukas.

"Sure," he agreed.

The door banged shut behind her, but then there was silence—and a whole lot of tension.

Kelly stirred a spoonful of sugar into her cup. "Did you get your paperwork done on the weekend?"

"Paperwork is never done," he told her.

"Then it wasn't just an excuse to avoid seeing me?"

"Believe it or not, not everything is about you. I had a busy life here while you were in Seattle, and it's still just as busy."

"And that's why I haven't heard from you in almost a week—because you've been busy?"

"Yeah."

She frowned at the terse response. "Have you talked to Jackson?"

"I think I said everything I needed to say to him."

Kelly sighed. "If you want to be mad at someone, you should be mad at me, not your brother."

"Don't worry," Lukas assured her. "I'm plenty mad at you, too."

"And you have every right to be," she admitted. "I should have told you."

He just stood with his arms folded across his chest and said nothing.

"I was going to tell you," she said, aware that she sounded more than a little defensive.

"When?" he demanded. "When *my niece* was graduating from college?"

She winced. "I hated keeping the truth from you."

"But you did it, anyway—for *thirteen years*."

"What was I supposed to do?" she challenged. "By the time I knew I was pregnant, Jack was engaged to Sara."

"He still had a right to know that you were going to have his child."

"And he would have been thrilled with me for ruining his wedding plans—and his career—wouldn't he?"

He lifted his brows at her sarcasm. "No, he probably

wouldn't have been thrilled. But he would have done the right thing."

"What was the right thing?"

"Marrying you and being a father to his child."

She shook her head. "And you couldn't guess why I didn't tell you?"

"He would have stepped up."

"Maybe. And then he would have hated me."

"You don't know that," he told her.

"He was in love with Sara."

"He probably thought he was, when he asked her to marry him," Lukas admitted. "But when she broke off the engagement, he told me that he was more relieved than anything, because he'd realized that the whole thing was a mistake."

"And yet he was happy enough to put the ring back on her finger when she changed her mind again."

He frowned at that. "I don't know what was going through his mind at the time, but I do know that he would have done things differently if he'd known that you were pregnant."

"I didn't want him to feel trapped by circumstances neither of us could have foreseen."

"You didn't give him a chance to feel anything."

She blinked back the tears that threatened. "You're right," she admitted. "Because I was pregnant and alone and so terrified I didn't think about his feelings. Or yours."

Now Lukas sighed. "I never understood why you refused to tell me. Now that part, at least, makes sense."

"Are you going to stay mad at me forever?" she asked softly.

He considered the question for a minute. "Probably not forever," he said. "And I wasn't only mad—I felt like an idiot."

"Why?"

"Because I never even suspected the truth. I never picked up on any vibes between you and Jack, and I never saw how much Ava looks like him."

"Jack doesn't see it, either," she said. "Or maybe he doesn't want to see it."

"Matt said he figured it out the first time he saw her, so it probably won't take other people too long to see the resemblance," he warned.

She knew he was right. "I'm going to tell her."

"When?"

"Soon," she assured him. "It's just that Ava's wanted a father for so long, I can't help but be a little concerned that, when she finally gets to meet him, she's going to expect too much."

"And you don't think Jack can live up to her expectations," he guessed.

"I don't know that he wants to." She sipped her coffee. "Maybe coming back to Pinehurst was a mistake."

"Do you really think so?"

"No," she admitted. "It was time to leave Seattle—and there wasn't anywhere else I wanted to go. Besides—" she nudged his shoulder "—I missed my best friend."

He shook his head. "You're making it really hard for me to stay mad at you."

"You have every right to be mad at me," she admitted.

"Even if I could understand why you didn't say anything in the beginning," he allowed, "I can't understand why you kept the truth of her paternity a secret for so long."

"Because I knew exactly how you'd react when you found out that your brother was Ava's father."

She didn't realize that Ava had come back into the house or overheard any part of the conversation with Lukas until her daughter said, "Dr. Garrett's my father?"

Chapter Seven

Jack was staring at his planner and trying to figure out what he was going to do with the four days he'd set aside for a contentious custody hearing that had been postponed. Ordinarily, he would have opposed the eleventh-hour adjournment request as prejudicial to his client, except in this situation, it was not. Because his client had interim custody of her three children and her estranged husband was currently in the custody of the Las Vegas Police Department after a weekend trip with some buddies ended with an ill-advised proposition to an undercover police officer.

He wasn't accustomed to so much unscheduled time. He enjoyed his work and he had no problem with fifteen-hour days or even working weekends. In fact, he sometimes worried that he wouldn't know what to do if he didn't have such a busy practice. And there were other times that he wished he could escape from his clients' problems, just for a little while. Now that he had such an opportunity, he thought he should focus on his own life—and establishing a relationship with his daughter.

He looked up at a knock on his door. "What are you still doing here?" he asked his secretary.

"I'm not still here," Colleen told him. "I went home for dinner, saw a movie with a friend, then came back to pick up some files I wanted to finish billing tonight. You're the only one *still* here."

"Not for long," he told her, shutting down his computer.

"Well, since you are here, you can let me know what to do about Norah Hennessey Sinclair. She called several times this afternoon demanding an appointment for tomorrow."

"And you said?"

"That you were scheduled to be in court all week, which is technically true."

"Your boss should give you a raise," Jack told her.

"He should," she agreed. "But he's way too cheap."

"Or he could demote you to the copy room."

She just shrugged, unconcerned. "If she calls again in the morning, do you want me to book her in for Monday morning? If I schedule an 8:00-a.m. appointment, she should be sober."

"I told you about that dinner meeting in confidence," he reminded her.

Colleen glanced around the empty office, but all she said was, "Monday?"

"The following Monday," he allowed. "I want to keep next week open."

"For what?"

"Personal reasons."

"You usually have to have a personal life to justify personal reasons," she pointed out.

"Ha, ha."

"I wasn't joking."

He closed the lid on his briefcase. "You know how to reach me in case of emergency."

"You're really taking time off?"

"And I have complete confidence that you can handle the office."

She folded her arms across her chest. "Who are you and what have you done with Jackson Garrett?"

He chuckled. "Go home, Colleen. You can do the billing tomorrow."

She was walking beside him to the elevator when his cell phone rang. Jack pulled it out of his pocket, surprised—and pleased—to see Kelly's name and number on the display.

"Maybe I was wrong about you not having a personal life," his secretary mused, punching the button to summon the elevator.

Jack connected the call as the elevator dinged to signal its arrival.

"I hope it's not too late," Kelly said without preamble.

"Actually, I'm just leaving the office," he told her.

"In that case, could you stop by on your way home?"

He couldn't resist teasing, "If this is a booty call—absolutely."

"In your dreams."

She had no idea how very true those words were. And while he had a ready retort on his lips, the underlying tension in her voice prompted him to ask instead, "Is everything okay?"

"Not really," she admitted.

"Ava?"

"She's fine, but—" She blew out a breath. "I'd really rather talk about this in person."

"I'll be there in ten minutes," he promised.

He was pulling into her driveway in less than that, and when Kelly answered the door, he could see the worry in her eyes.

"What's going on?"

She managed a wobbly smile. "Well, you said that you wanted Ava to know—now she knows."

He did want Ava to know, but he'd got the impression that Kelly was a little less eager to share the news, so this revelation coming so soon on the heels of their earlier conversation surprised him. "You told her?"

"She overheard Lukas and I talking." She hesitated, as if she was going to say something else, then apparently changed her mind.

"How did she take it?" he asked cautiously.

"She didn't say too much on the drive home," Kelly admitted. "And then she went to her room and slammed the door."

"Is she mad at you or me?"

"Both, I'd guess, but probably more at me. She thinks I should have told her who her father was a long time ago."

He couldn't disagree, so instead he asked, "Why am I here?"

"I don't know," she admitted. "I probably shouldn't have called. I thought maybe you could talk to her, but I don't think she's in a mood to listen to anyone right now."

When he'd suggested telling Ava about their relationship, he'd assumed that he and Kelly would sit down together and make the announcement. But he hadn't anticipated what kind of reaction Ava might have to the news, and he certainly hadn't expected to be called in for damage control. Or to worry that he might exacerbate the damage.

"I can try," he said, and she looked up at him, her golden eyes filled with wary hope and reluctant gratitude.

He climbed the stairs to the second floor. Even if he hadn't known which room was Ava's, he could have guessed by the firmly closed door. He knocked, but the sound barely registered over the pounding of his heart against his ribs.

"Go away."

He turned the knob, pushed open the door a crack.

She glared at him from her cross-legged position in the middle of her bed. "I said 'go away.'"

"I thought maybe that was code for something else—like how 'sick' actually means 'cool.'"

"You thought wrong."

He shrugged. "Do you want to tell me why you're so pissed off at me?"

Her jaw dropped. "You're not supposed to swear in front of me."

"Why not?"

"Because I'm a kid and it sets a bad example," she informed him primly.

He stepped farther into the room, straddled the ladder-back chair at her desk. "I don't have a lot of experience with kids," he admitted.

"Could've fooled me." Her voice dripped with sarcasm, but at least she was talking to him.

"So why are you pi—mad at me?" he asked again.

She held a fuzzy purple pillow against her chest, her fingers raking through the fur as she considered how to respond—or maybe if she should. Instead of answering his question, she asked one of her own. "Did you sleep with my mom and then dump her?"

"Is that what she told you?"

"I didn't ask her," Ava admitted. "I'm asking you."

"You could have started with an easier question," he grumbled.

She hugged the pillow tighter and waited for his response.

Jack knew he could try to slant the truth in his favor, but what would be the point? It seemed as if Ava had already made up her mind about him and nothing he said was going to change it.

"Yeah," he finally said. "That's not a complete summary of what happened, but it's basically accurate."

"Did you know she was pregnant?"

"No." Kelly answered her daughter's question from the doorway before he could. "When we decided to go our separate ways, neither of us knew that I was pregnant."

"Didn't they teach you about safe sex back then?"

Thankfully, Kelly came to his rescue again, adeptly skirting the question as she lowered herself onto the edge of her daughter's bed. "Just because you weren't planned doesn't mean you weren't wanted."

"Maybe you wanted me," Ava acknowledged. "But what about him?"

"That's not a fair question," Kelly chided. "Because I moved to Seattle without telling Jack about you."

"Why?"

"It's…complicated."

"Don't you think I have a right to know why I didn't have a father for the first twelve years of my life?"

"The details don't matter as much as the fact that you have a father now."

Ava looked at him with blatant skepticism. "Do I?"

"I know this revelation came as a surprise to you—it was a surprise to me, too," he admitted. "And I'm not expecting you to embrace me with open arms, but I'm hoping that we can give each other a chance to try and figure this out."

She didn't seem thrilled with the idea, and finally admitted, "I thought Dr. Garrett was my father."

Jack glanced at Kelly in surprise and confusion; she shrugged apologetically.

"Mom told Uncle Lukas that his brother was my father," Ava explained. "And I thought—I *hoped*—she meant Dr. Garrett."

"Matt already has three kids," he said lightly.

"Probably because he likes kids."

He frowned. "I like kids."

She rolled her eyes. "I might only be twelve, but I'm not stupid."

"Ava," Kelly said warningly.

But the child kept her gaze firmly on Jack. "How long have you known about me?"

He cleared his throat. "Your mom told me last week."

"And you were obviously overjoyed."

"I was...overwhelmed," he said cautiously.

"Did you ever plan to have kids?"

He glanced to Kelly for assistance, but she looked as helpless as he felt. "I never thought too much about the possibility," he finally acknowledged.

"I guess I know now why Mom didn't tell you about me," Ava said. "Because she knew you wouldn't want me."

"That's not true," Jack said.

"And not fair," Kelly interjected.

"Isn't it?" She tossed the pillow aside and pushed off the bed to face him more directly. "What did you say when she told you about me?"

"Ava," Kelly said, trying to divert her attention.

She shook her head. "I want to know."

Jack held her gaze. "I didn't react well," he admitted.

Green eyes, so similar to his own, narrowed. "You didn't want to believe it, did you? That's why Dr. Turcotte took that swab—it wasn't a strep test but a DNA test."

"I don't doubt that you're my daughter," Jack said now, because it was true.

"Did you ask for a DNA test?" Ava asked.

He sighed. "Yes."

Her eyes filled with tears. Then she turned on her heel and stormed out of the room and down the hall to slam another door.

Kelly blew out a breath. "Look at us—one big happy family."

"At least now I know where she gets her penchant for sarcasm." He scrubbed his hands over his face. "I completely screwed that up, didn't I?"

"Welcome to parenthood." Kelly stood up and moved toward the door.

Jack followed. "Maybe if you'd said those words twelve years ago, I might have figured out a few things by now," he told her. "Instead, you spring a twelve-year-old child on me and I have no idea what to say or do."

"I was just as unprepared to be a parent when she was born," Kelly reminded him as she made her way down the stairs. "And completely on my own."

"That was your choice," he shot back.

"I never chose to be a single parent," she argued. "I only chose not to tell your fiancée that I was pregnant with your baby. And truthfully, when I realized that you'd jumped from my bed right back to hers, I decided that you weren't the kind of man I wanted as a father to my child."

The accusation wasn't just hurtful, it was wrong. "I didn't jump from your bed to hers," he protested.

"When you came to Chicago, you told me your engagement was over. And when I called you a few months later, *she* answered your phone."

"We weren't together when I came to Chicago." He paced the length of the living room. "God, Kelly, how could you even think otherwise? There's no way I would have spent that weekend with you if I'd still been with Sara."

"So when did you get back together with her?" she wanted to know. "The day after you got back from Chicago?"

"You'd like to believe that, wouldn't you? Because then I'm the bad guy and you can feel self-righteous about keeping my child from me for the past twelve years."

"Are you denying that's what happened?"

"It's not even close to what happened."

She shook her head. "It doesn't matter."

"The only reason I even agreed to see Sara again is that I couldn't stop thinking about you."

"That's your story? That you jumped into bed with your ex because you were thinking about me?"

He heard the scorn in her voice and knew he couldn't blame her for being skeptical. Looking at the situation now, he could see that it wasn't the most logical course of action. But at the time, it was the only option he could see.

"Yeah, because no other woman has ever haunted me the way you did. After only three days together, I couldn't stop thinking about you. Even weeks later, you were my first thought in the morning and my last thought at night. And I couldn't think about you without wanting you. It's never been that way before, not with anyone else. So when Sara called, I wanted to believe that I wasn't missing you specifically, I was just missing being with someone." He pinned her with his gaze. "I was wrong."

"And yet, a few months later, you married her."

"I knew it was probably a mistake," he acknowledged. "But I knew that if I chased after you, I'd be making a bigger one."

She drew in a sharp breath and rubbed a hand over her breastbone, as if to assuage an ache, and he cursed himself for hurting her yet again when that was exactly what he'd tried to avoid from the beginning.

"Well, that's a flattering assessment."

He scrubbed his hands over his face. "It would have been a mistake because the timing was all wrong. Dammit, Kelly, I didn't want you sacrificing your education or your career because you thought you were in love with me."

"I did think I was in love with you," she agreed. "But I fell out of love quickly enough when reality hit."

"You're never going to forgive me for what happened thirteen years ago, are you?"

"On the contrary, I'm grateful to you for what happened thirteen years ago, for giving me Ava."

"But you can't forgive me for not being there for you—even though I didn't know there was any reason to be there."

"And if you had known? If I'd responded to the news of your engagement with 'That's great, Jack—you're getting married and you're going to be a father,' what would you have done?"

"I don't know," he admitted.

"I do," she told him. "You would have freaked because my unplanned pregnancy could have destroyed everything you wanted—not just your relationship with Sara but your name on the door of her father's law firm."

"Maybe I would have," he acknowledged. "I was young and stupid—and no way was I prepared to be a parent."

She just nodded. There was no need for her to point out again that she had been even younger and equally unprepared to be a parent. And yet she'd done what she needed to do.

"What about now?" she asked.

"I don't feel any more prepared now," he admitted. "Why do you think I panicked when you told me about Ava? Maybe part of it was that I wasn't ready to believe she was my child, but a bigger part was because I don't know how to be a father. But...I want to try."

She nodded again. "Thank you."

"You probably shouldn't thank me just yet," he warned.

"You have your faults, Jacks, but I've never known you to give up on something just because it wasn't easy. And Ava really needs a father."

* * *

Kelly didn't push her daughter to make conversation the next morning. After everything that had happened the night before, she figured Ava was entitled to be quiet and introspective, but she was hopeful that a day at camp would improve her mood. That hope was short-lived as Ava barely spoke half a dozen words on the way home at the end of the day, and those were only in response to direct questions.

"How was camp today?"

"Fine."

"What did you do?"

"The usual."

"What was for lunch today?"

"Cold pizza."

"Is Laurel going back next week?"

"Yeah."

Thankfully it wasn't a very long drive from camp to home, so while the silence the rest of the way was awkward, it wasn't interminable. And then she turned onto Larkspur Drive and saw a familiar vehicle parked in front of the house.

Ava apparently recognized the vehicle, too, because her scowl darkened. But she said nothing, only grabbed her backpack and slammed out of the car. Kelly unlocked the house for her, then waited on the driveway for Jackson.

He didn't look like he'd come from the office today. Instead of a shirt and tie, he was dressed in a pair of jeans and a T-shirt. But he still looked good. Too good.

The surprise must have shown on her face, because the first words he spoke were "Did you forget you invited me to dinner?"

"No, I just thought, after Ava's reaction last night, you might not want to come back here."

"I didn't expect it was going to be easy. I hoped it might be," he admitted, with just the hint of a smile. "But I didn't expect it."

"It could be a quiet meal—Ava's barely talking to me."

"She can't give us the silent treatment forever."

"You might be surprised," Kelly warned. "She's stubborn and hardheaded. Which I guess only proves she's a Garrett."

"Yeah, because you're such a pushover," he said dryly.

She had to smile at that. "How do you feel about fajitas?"

"As favorably as I feel about any meal that someone else is making," he assured her.

"It's one of Ava's favorites," she told him. "Tacos are the absolute number one, but we just had those last week."

"And you're still feeling guilty for the way she found out about me," he guessed.

"I've been feeling guilty for twelve years." She opened the fridge to pull out the ingredients she'd chopped earlier that morning.

While she started cooking, Jack opened the bottle of wine he'd brought. "And in those twelve years," he said, "did you ever think about contacting me?"

She nodded. "From the day she was born, and for a long time after, I thought about it almost every day. But you were married to Sara, then I married Malcolm, and then it seemed as if I'd let it go for too long."

He poured the wine into two glasses. "When was she born? All you told me was that it was February, but you didn't mention the actual date."

She added the onions and peppers to the pan. "The twelfth."

"February twelfth," he echoed. And she could tell by his tone that he finally understood why she hadn't reached out to him on that day.

She nodded. "Ava was born the day you got married."

* * *

When they sat down to eat and Ava finally decided to break her self-imposed vow of silence, the first words out of her mouth were "I've decided that I should move in with Jack."

Kelly had to focus all of her effort on breathing. Suddenly there was an unbearable weight on her chest that made it impossible to draw air into her lungs. She didn't know if Ava's request to live with Jack was based on a desire to get to know him better or a plan to punish her mother for keeping the identity of her father a secret for so long; she only knew that her heart was breaking into a thousand pieces.

Maybe she should have anticipated this. Or maybe, subconsciously, this scenario was one of the reasons she'd stayed in Washington as long as she had. Because she'd feared that when Ava found her father, she'd choose to be with him. Because no one had ever chosen Kelly. Not her mother or her father, not even the man she married, and certainly not Jackson. So why should she expect her daughter to be any different?

He seemed to recover from his surprise first. "You want to live…with me?"

Ava nodded.

His panicked gaze flew across the table, but Kelly couldn't help him. She was still too busy trying to process her daughter's statement to know what to do or say.

"Where is this coming from?" Jackson finally asked.

"I was talking to Laurel about the fact that I suddenly have this father I don't even know, and she suggested that the best way to get to know you would be to live with you."

Kelly managed to find her voice. "You talked to Laurel about this?"

"Yeah." Ava lifted her chin. "So?"

"So…I thought we might want to take some time to think about this before we announced it to the whole world."

"I didn't announce it to the world—I told my one and only friend in Pinetar, and you can't get mad at me because I know you've at least told Uncle Lukas."

Which, of course, she couldn't dispute. "You're right. And I'm glad you have a friend in whom you feel comfortable confiding, but living with Jackson is not an option."

"Why not?"

"Because I've only got a one-bedroom apartment," he said.

"I can sleep on the couch," Ava offered.

"Actually, it's an adults-only complex."

"What does that mean?"

"It means that no one has kids."

She frowned. "Why would you live in a place like that?"

"It's a nice building in a good location." He shrugged. "And there was no reason not to live there, because I never had a kid before now."

"I know you're eager to spend time with Jack," Kelly said, trying to keep her tone calm and rational, "but this situation is new to all of us and I think we should, right now, just take it one day at a time."

Ava didn't seem thrilled with this suggestion, but she turned her attention back to her plate. She finished folding her second tortilla and took a bite, and Kelly exhaled a quiet sigh.

"I noticed a picture of you in a soccer uniform in the living room," Jack commented when she was finished eating. "Do you still play?"

"Not this year," Ava told him, with another unhappy look toward her mother. "I couldn't do anything this summer because we were moving."

"You've been playing at camp," Kelly reminded her.

"Like that counts," the girl grumbled.

"There's a school tournament every fall," Jackson interjected. "Tryouts for the team start the second week of September."

"I'm really rusty," Ava said.

"Do you have a ball?" Jack asked.

"Of course I have a ball."

"Then why don't we take it outside and see just how rusty you are?" he suggested.

Ava looked at him as if he'd just offered her the moon on a silver platter. "Do *you* play?"

"Just for fun every once in a while now," he told her. "But I was on the varsity team all through high school and I usually help Adam Webber—he's the fifth-grade teacher and coach of the girls' team—with his practices."

Ava was already pushing away from the table. Then she suddenly remembered the manners that had been ingrained in her and paused to ask, "May I be excused?"

Kelly nodded. "Go wash up."

Ava carried her plate and cup to the counter, then raced up the stairs. Ordinarily Kelly would have called her back to put her dishes *in* the dishwasher, but she was so grateful to Jackson for successfully diffusing the volatile situation that she wasn't going to object to being stuck with the kitchen cleanup.

"She's good," Kelly told Jack as she started carrying the rest of the dishes to the sink. "You won't have to use your personal connection with the coach to get her on the team."

"I expect her to be good," Jack said, with more than a hint of arrogance. "She's my kid."

"Yeah, all I did was carry her in my womb for nine months and give birth after thirty-four hours of labor," Kelly noted dryly.

His cocky smile faded. "Thirty-four hours?"

"Actually, it was only four hours," she admitted, her own lips curving. "But no one ever sympathizes with a woman who only suffers through four hours of hard labor."

He turned her around to face him, his expression serious now. "Was it hard?"

"Not really. It was a pretty routine pregnancy and a blessedly quick birth. But the twelve years since have definitely been a challenge."

Before he could say anything else, Ava was back with her ball in hand.

Kelly tried to focus on the dishes while Jackson and Ava kicked the ball around the backyard, but she couldn't prevent her gaze from occasionally shifting toward the window. Ava's earlier moodiness was completely forgotten, and she was smiling and laughing as she deked around Jack. But he had some pretty good moves of his own for a thirty-seven-year-old, and sometimes their battles for control were pretty intense. Certainly Jack didn't seem to be trying to score any points with his daughter by letting her win.

It was the sound of barking that drew her attention to the window again, and she saw that the game had expanded now to include Matt, Quinn and Shane, with Finnigan and Frederick trying to chase the ball and avoid flying feet.

There didn't seem to be any real purpose to the action, at least not so far as Kelly could tell. But they were all laughing and having a great time, and she felt as if some of the enormous weight had been lifted off of her chest as she watched her daughter playing with her father.

She hadn't been sure it would ever happen. Even when she'd decided to return to Pinehurst, she couldn't have predicted what would happen when Ava and Jack each learned about the other. And although she knew there would inevitably be bumps further down the road, this, at least, had turned out to be a very good day.

Chapter Eight

On Saturday, Jack invited Ava and Kelly to go hiking at Eagle Point Park. He didn't know if either of them was the outdoorsy type, but it was a perfect day to be outside, as evidenced by the numerous other groups and families on the trails. The sky was a brilliant blue and nearly cloudless, and though the sun was high in the sky when they started, the canopy of trees offered some respite from the heat.

There hadn't been much rain in the past couple of weeks, so the trail was dry, the dirt packed hard from all the boots and shoes that had stomped upon it. Sometimes, if he wasn't in a hurry, Jack would look for animal tracks, but he knew they wouldn't find any today.

They started along one of the easier routes with the thought that a less strenuous hike might help facilitate conversation. But after a brief discussion of the weather and an even briefer discussion about the local flora and fauna, Ava plugged in her earbuds. Obviously she preferred her music to the sounds of nature—and conversation with her parents.

After a few minutes, Kelly said, "Lukas never told me that you coached soccer."

"I'm not actually the coach—I just help out."

"Still, I would have thought that a man who'd shared that basic connection with kids wouldn't freak out at the news that he had a kid of his own."

"But they weren't kids to me," he admitted. "They were

soccer players. And if I ever did think of them as kids, there was comfort in knowing they were someone else's."

"Are you still freaked out?"

"No. Just terrified."

She smiled. "Good."

"Why is that good?"

"Because you wouldn't be scared if you didn't care. It proves that she matters to you."

"I didn't expect that she would matter so much so fast," he admitted. "I mean, I barely had my head around the fact that I was a father and suddenly she was *my* child."

To his surprise, Kelly's eyes filled with tears.

"What did I do?" he asked warily.

She shook her head. "You said 'my child' without any hesitation."

"Yeah, well." He wasn't quite sure how to respond to that.

Kelly laughed. "So what have you been doing with your life besides practicing law and helping-but-not-coaching girls' soccer?"

He was grateful for the change of topic. "Work doesn't leave me a lot of time for anything else."

"How long have you been on your own?"

Obviously she knew that he was practicing independently now, because she'd been to his office and the name "Taylor & Ross" wasn't on the door. He thought Lukas might have told her the details of his decision to leave his father-in-law's firm, but maybe she'd never asked about him, as he'd been careful not to ask his brother about her.

"Almost ten years," he said in response to her question.

She stopped in the middle of the path. "You left Taylor and Ross ten years ago?"

"Yeah. About two years before Sara left me."

"Why?"

"Because I did want my name on the door, but I wanted to know that I'd earned it. As long as I was working for my father-in-law, I would never be sure."

"I'm sorry," she said. "For that crack I made about it being a wedding present."

"I'm a lawyer," he reminded her. "You'd have to throw sharper barbs than that to pierce my thick skin."

"I'll keep that in mind."

"How about you? What have you been doing with your life besides cooking books and raising our daughter?"

"Forensic accountants don't cook books," she said indignantly. "They investigate and analyze financial evidence."

"And they have very thin skin." As if to prove the point, he rubbed his hand on her upper arm briskly. He was being playful, teasing her. But then he noticed that her skin wasn't thin, but soft, and warm. And his movements slowed, gentled.

She stepped away, picked up her pace. "But my new job is more managerial than practical, and my hours will be more regular, which means I'll be able to spend less time at work and more time with Ava."

Jack fell into step beside her again.

"But speaking of cooking books," she continued in a deliberately casual tone. "I do have a collection of cookbooks that I haven't cracked open in far too long because I didn't have time for anything more than the basics, and I think I'd like to start cooking again for fun."

"I thought cooking was just for eating," he admitted. "And speaking of eating—why don't we stop for lunch when we get to Summit Falls?"

So they did.

Kelly had offered to pack a lunch, but Jack had arranged for a takeout picnic from the Bean There Café. A pointed look from her mother had Ava tucking her music away while they dined on turkey sandwiches, macaroni salad and potato chips, and washed it all down with bottles of water. But as soon as they were packing up to head back to the trail, the music came out again.

Obviously, Ava wasn't a nature lover, but Jack wasn't too disappointed. His plans for the day hadn't been a complete bust, because at least he and Kelly seemed to be communicating again. He wasn't ready to forgive her entirely—and he didn't doubt that she still had some residual anger of her own to work through—but he was at least confident that they could cooperate for the sake of their daughter.

Based on the experience at Eagle Point Park, Jack suspected that the urban jungle might be more Ava's style. So the following day, he decided to take her to The Fun Warehouse in Syracuse. He extended the invitation to Kelly as well, but he wasn't surprised when she declined, claiming that she had errands to run. As much as he enjoyed spending time with both of them, he couldn't deny that being close to his daughter's mother was more than a little distracting. Especially when he couldn't stop thinking about the kiss they'd shared in her kitchen more than a week earlier.

He picked Ava up at ten o'clock and took her to The Pancake Palace to fuel up on carbs before they went gaming. They played three rounds of laser tag and five games of air hockey (three of which she won), and then spent an hour in the arcade, at the conclusion of which they were both suffering from extreme sensory overload. But when they got back to Pinehurst, it was still only early afternoon.

"Are you ready to go home? Or do you want to check out my condo?"

"Am I allowed?" she asked hesitantly.

"There are no age restrictions on visitors."

"Okay."

He parked in his usual spot and led her into the building. She looked around curiously, but didn't say anything. In fact, as they made their way toward the bank of elevators, she seemed to be tiptoeing.

"It's so quiet," she said, her voice pitched so low it was practically inaudible. "I feel like I'm in a library."

"That's because you're whispering," he said, speaking in a normal tone.

"I don't want to get you in trouble for having a kid in the no-kid zone."

"The official designation is adult lifestyle condominium," he reminded her.

"We lived in a condo in Seattle," she told him. "On the twelfth floor. What floor are you on?"

"Three," he said, and pressed the button for his floor.

She frowned at the panel. "There are only three floors?"

"This isn't Seattle," he reminded her.

"No kidding," she grumbled.

She shrugged and wandered through the living room, studying the art on his walls, the books on his shelf, the CD collection. Then she wandered over to the floor-to-ceiling windows, peered out. "There's no Space Needle, but the view doesn't completely suck."

"High praise," he mused. "Do you miss Washington?"

She lifted a shoulder. "I miss my friends."

"You've already made some new friends, haven't you?"

"Yeah. A few. At camp."

"Are you looking forward to starting school?"

She just shrugged. "I'm thinking of getting some more streaks in my hair before then. Maybe green this time."

Jack shook his head, genuinely baffled. "Why would you cover up such pretty hair with fake color?"

"You think my hair's pretty?"

"It's beautiful," he told her sincerely. "You're beautiful." Because she was, and it absolutely stunned and humbled him to know that she was his daughter, that he'd had any part in the creation of this gorgeous creature. "Did you know you look just like your mother did at the same age?"

"Really?"

He nodded. "In fact, I think she was just a couple of years younger than you are now when she first came to live with her grandmother in Pinehurst."

"Have you known her since then?" she asked curiously.

"Yeah. Although I didn't know her very well. She and Lukas were always best buddies, though."

"When did you start to like her?"

Jack realized, too late, that he'd started a conversation he wasn't sure he wanted to finish. Because he knew that when she asked about him "liking" her mother she wasn't referring to the platonic friendship sort of "like" but the boy-and-girl-get-naked-together-and-make-a-baby sort. For purposes of self-preservation, however, he pretended to misunderstand. "I always got along okay with your mom."

Ava rolled her eyes. "When did you start to date her?"

That one wouldn't be deflected quite so easily, but it was even more awkward for Jack to answer because the truth was, he and Kelly had never really dated. They'd flirted, they'd kissed, and then they'd jumped into bed together without ever having been out on a single date.

"Not until she was in college."

"I thought she went to college in Chicago."

"She did," he confirmed.

She nodded, as if that explained everything. "Long-distance romances never work."

"And you know this—how?"

"Regan—Rachel's sister. Her boyfriend went to UCLA, which isn't even really that far from Seattle. But he said he had to break up with her because missing her was interfering with his schoolwork. Regan said it was sleeping with all the L.A. sluts that was interfering with his schoolwork." Ava shrugged. "Either way, she's got a new boyfriend now."

The matter-of-fact tone in which she'd referenced sex unnerved him as much as the content. She was *twelve,* for God's sake. He tried to think back, to remember what he'd known about sex at the same age, and came up with nothing. Which probably was the answer.

Apparently Seattle was a world away from Pinehurst in more than distance. And what kind of comment was he supposed to make now to follow up that revelation? He didn't have a clue.

"Are you hungry?" he asked, in a desperate and not-at-all subtle attempt to change the topic of conversation.

"Yeah."

"Do you want to go out to eat or help me make dinner here?"

"You cook?"

She sounded so dubious, he had to smile. "Well enough that I don't starve."

"What can you make?"

"Fettuccine, linguine, spaghettini, tortellini."

Ava rolled her eyes. "So basically you know how to boil water and cook pasta?"

"I can also make tacos."

"In that case," she decided, "let's eat here."

While Jack browned and seasoned the ground beef, Ava chopped lettuce and tomatoes and grated the cheese.

"Hard or soft shell?" he asked, setting a plate with both on the table.

"Soft," she replied, automatically reaching for one. "Hard are too messy."

"There's a trick to eating hard tacos," he told her, spooning filling into his shell.

She expertly rolled up her tortilla. "What's that?"

"The grip." He held the top of the shell with his fingers, then brought the taco to his mouth and bit into the end.

The shell broke apart and dumped all the meat and toppings onto his plate.

Ava giggled.

"And then," Jack continued, as if the disintegration of his taco had been planned all along, "you use your fork to scoop up the rest."

"I'll have to try that next time," she said gamely.

Then she neatly bit into her own taco.

It wasn't unusual for Ava to be up early on the first day of school. But this year, Kelly suspected that her daughter's inability to sleep in was as much apprehension as anticipation. It was seventh grade so the whole school thing was hardly new to her, but it was a new school, and Kelly remembered all too clearly how difficult that could be.

Ava was seated at the breakfast bar now, dressed in a new pair of jeans and a peasant-style top, with her purple-painted toenails peeking out of her sandals. She pushed her Cheerios around in her bowl, stirring more than eating.

Yeah, Kelly remembered first-day jitters.

She took a sip her coffee. "Do you want me to take you to school?"

Ava looked up from her cereal with an expression of absolute horror. "I'd rather wear a neon sign flashing 'new kid' over my head."

"That's a better idea," she agreed. "But I don't know where we'd find one this early in the morning."

Her daughter pushed away from the table.

"Brush your teeth," she said, because she'd been saying it for so many years it had become a habit.

Ava rolled her eyes. "Cuz that would never have occurred to me."

Kelly chose to ignore the sarcasm because she knew that Ava was dealing with a lot. Not just her first day at a new school, but settling into a new home in a new town, and getting to know her father. While there hadn't been too many bumps in the road and nothing too major, she had to be feeling overwhelmed. Anxious. Uncertain.

Or maybe Kelly was projecting her own feelings onto her daughter.

When Ava returned from the bathroom and lifted her backpack onto her shoulder, Kelly indulged herself by stroking a hand down her daughter's hair. The purple streaks had almost completely faded and her hair was soft and silky. "You look very nice."

Ava smiled shyly. "Thanks."

Kelly kissed her forehead. "I'll be here when you get home," she promised. "But just in case, you know where the key is, don't you?"

"Yes, I know where the key is."

Kelly kissed her cheek. "Have a good day."

"You, too."

She stood at the front window, watching her walk down the sidewalk and trying not to worry.

A few minutes later, she was on her way out to the car when she saw Georgia making her way down the sidewalk, flanked by Shane and Quinn with matching packs on their backs. Matt was right behind them, with the baby strapped in a carrier on his chest. The twins' first day of school was obviously a whole family event, and Kelly couldn't deny that she felt just a little bit envious as she watched them set off.

Ava's first day had been an entirely different experience, as was the case with most of her daughter's firsts. Kelly had been there, of course, as had Bev, but the little girl's father had been three thousand miles away and unable to share any of those milestone moments with her. And while Kelly sometimes regretted that fact, she'd managed to convince herself that she'd made the right choice. That even if Jack had known about his child, he had hardly been the type to hold her tiny hand in his on that long walk to the first day of school.

Now she wasn't so sure. And she felt a pang of regret that she'd denied him—and Ava—that opportunity.

One of the greatest perks of Kelly's new job was the flexible hours. Craig Richmond might have been the company vice president, but he was also a father of four, and he assured her that she wouldn't have to punch a clock. He didn't care if she arrived late or left early so long as the work got done. Kelly decided to take him at his word and tried not to feel guilty about leaving work at two o'clock so that she would be home before Ava got back from her first day at school.

Apparently Jackson didn't have to punch a clock, either, because he was on her front step when she pulled into the driveway, and her heart automatically did a little skip and jump. She found it as baffling as it was frustrating that he continued to have such an effect on her. After everything they'd been through and in spite of the current tension and distrust between them, just a hint of his smile was enough to make her knees weak.

"For you," he said, handing her a paper-wrapped bundle of roses and daisies and freesia. "To commemorate Ava's first day of school."

"You mean her first day in the seventh grade?"

He shrugged. "Sure."

Though she was still a little puzzled, she brought the bouquet up to her nose and inhaled the fragrant scent of the blossoms. "Thank you."

"I've been thinking about all of the things I missed out on because I didn't know about Ava. And as much as I'm angry and frustrated that I'll never get that time back, I realized that I at least have an opportunity to get to know my daughter now. And although I don't know her very well, I know that she's a good kid. And that's because of you."

She had to blink away tears as she unlocked the door. "That was quite the speech."

"I practiced while I waited for you to come home. I've been here since about ten o'clock this morning."

She smiled at the blatant fib. "Don't you have a job?"

"One of the perks of being my own boss is that I can take a day off if I want to. Unless I'm scheduled to be in court or have a client emergency," he amended.

She filled a vase with water, arranged the flowers in it. "Well, I'm glad you could be here today. I know Ava will be happy to see you when she gets home. But she'll probably be tired," she warned. "She never sleeps very well the night before the first day."

"Do you remember her very first day?" he asked.

"As if it was yesterday."

"Can you tell me about it?"

"I can do a little better than that," she said, and went to the cabinet in the living room to pull out a photo album.

Jackson sat on the sofa and she opened the front cover of the book before setting it on the table in front of him.

"She was as cute as a button, wasn't she?" he said, pride evident in his tone.

"And terrified. You can tell by the way she's smiling— just a little too wide and bright. That was Ava putting on her brave face." She settled beside him. "She picked out her Dora lunchbox, and we packed it together. A cheese sandwich cut into four triangles with the crust removed, homemade chocolate chip cookies, apple wedges and fruit punch.

"Today, she took a couple of slices of leftover pizza, a package of cheesy crackers and a can of lemonade in a brown paper bag."

"What a difference eight years makes."

She nodded and pointed to another photo with a two-story brick building in the background. "That was her school." She turned the page. "And there's Ava with her teacher, Miss Watson."

"Did you stay and take pictures through the whole day?" he teased.

"No," Kelly admitted. "I dropped her off at school and headed to work, but I left my camera with Bev and she hung around for a while."

"She was your daycare provider?"

"As well as my neighbor, one of my first friends in Seattle, and eventually my mother-in-law."

"Is that how you met him…your husband?"

She nodded. "Bev never actually admitted it, but I think she kept setting things up to ensure our paths would cross. Calling Malcolm to come over on the nights she'd invite Ava and I to stay for dinner. Offering to watch Ava so I could attend various school functions with Malcolm."

"And eventually you fell in love," he guessed, keeping his gaze focused on the photo album.

"Yeah. Or close enough that we thought we could make marriage work."

"So what happened?" He felt compelled to ask, though he wasn't sure he wanted to know. Aside from the fact that the details of her marriage were none of his business, he couldn't stand the thought of Kelly with anyone else.

He knew it was completely irrational, but that knowledge didn't negate the feeling.

"He was offered a job in Boston—a very prestigious position at a private school—and I didn't want to leave Seattle."

He lifted his gaze to look at Kelly. "You got divorced because you didn't want to move?"

"I know it sounds ridiculous," she acknowledged. "But our difference of opinion on the job was only a symptom of a bigger problem, starting with the fact that he never asked what I wanted. He never even discussed the job offer with me before he accepted it. I was just supposed to be the dutiful little wife and start packing, never mind that I had a career of my own and a child to think about."

"He obviously didn't know you very well if he expected you to be a dutiful anything," Jack teased.

She smiled, though he could see the lingering sadness in her eyes. "And ultimately that was the truth," she agreed. "We each had our own reasons for marrying, but we didn't really know one another at all."

"That's not so different than what happened with me and Sara," he confided.

"She wanted you to move to Boston?"

He smiled. "No, but we each had our own reasons for marrying, and none of them were what they should have been."

Kelly didn't say anything, and really, what was there to say? What was the purpose in trying to explain what had gone wrong in his marriage when she wouldn't believe it anyway?

Only a complete fool married one woman when he was all tangled up in knots over another, and that's exactly what Jack had done.

"This is a picture of Bev with Ava." She pointed to another photo. "On a class trip to the Museum of Flight."

He flipped through more pages, enjoying more glimpses of Ava's first year at school. Marching in her first Halloween costume parade, creating her first handprint Thanksgiving turkey decoration, singing in her first Christmas pageant.

"Bev took most of those pictures," Kelly admitted. "I tried to be there as much as I could, but when I couldn't, she was."

"You miss her," he noted.

She nodded. "She was a good friend to me, and the closest thing to a grandmother that Ava's ever known." She looked at him now, her eyes filled with regret. "I didn't realize, when I decided to move to Washington, that your parents wouldn't ever have a chance to know their granddaughter. That Ava wouldn't have a chance to know them."

"They would have been over the moon to know they had a grandchild."

"And my parents have as little interest in Ava as they had in me."

He frowned at that. "I always thought…"

"You thought I lived with my grandmother because my parents were dead?"

He nodded.

"Nope. They just didn't want me."

"I'm sure that's not true."

"It is true," she said, in a neutral tone. "Both my parents are alive and well, and I haven't seen either of them in years. My mom lives in Australia with her third husband—she's never even met Ava. And my dad's a long-distance trucker with his home base in Detroit. He's only seen her a handful of times, although he usually remembers to send a card on her birthday."

"What about your birthday?" he asked.

She just shook her head.

I'd rather she didn't know the identity of her father than to know that he doesn't want to be her father.

At the time, her words had made no sense to Jack. Now he realized that she'd been speaking from personal experience, and it gave him some insight into her actions. Not that the neglect of her parents justified what she'd done, but it helped to explain it. Kelly's fear that he wouldn't want to be involved in his daughter's life wasn't so much a judgment against him but a response to her parents' lack of involvement in her own.

He finished thumbing through the album, ending with the little girl's kindergarten graduation, then closed the cover. "Do you have any pictures of Ava as a baby?"

She smiled. "Only about ten thousand."

"Then we should probably get started."

They were still poring over photo albums when Ava got home from school.

The envelope from PDA Labs was in his mail slot when he got home later that night. Until that moment, Jack had actually forgotten that he'd asked for the test. Well, demanded was more accurate, he acknowledged as he tore open the flap. His fingers weren't entirely steady as he pulled out the report and scanned for the result.

Probability of paternity: 99.99999%

He hadn't realized he was holding his breath until all of the air whooshed out of his lungs.

It was the most positive result that could be reported, and it confirmed beyond a shadow of a doubt that Ava was his daughter. Not that he had any doubt. Not after spending time with Kelly and Ava. But it was still a relief to have official confirmation in hand.

And he was relieved. When he'd first asked for the test, he'd been panicked, in denial. Kids were nowhere in his plan. No, thank you. Not interested in going down that road.

But he wasn't the type to shirk his responsibilities, and when he'd started to accept the possibility that he'd fathered a child, he'd resolved to do the right thing. He'd never suspected that he'd get to know the child and *want* to be her father. And he definitely hadn't anticipated that he would start reminiscing about his relationship with the child's mother.

Now, only a couple of weeks after Kelly's first visit to his office, everything had changed. He wanted the world to know that Ava was his.

And he was starting to realize that he wanted Kelly to be his, too.

Chapter Nine

Tryouts for the soccer team started the following week, each day for an hour after school with the first cuts being made on Wednesday. Jack was there every day to help Adam run drills and evaluate the players, as he'd been doing in each of the past few years. But this was the first year he had a vested interest in any of the students who were trying out for the team.

When practice was finished and Ava picked up her backpack, he went over to her. "Adam said there's no tryout tomorrow night because of something going on at the school."

"Yeah, it's a Meet the Teacher thing for parents."

"What's a 'Meet the Teacher thing'?"

"It's where parents go to the school…and meet the teacher."

"Should I go?"

"Do you want to go?"

Apparently they were both playing their cards close to the vest. He decided to lay his hand on the table. "Yes, I would like to go to your school to meet your teacher."

She blinked at the unequivocal response. "Really?"

"Unless you don't want me to go."

"No, I want you to go," she said. "If you want to go."

"What time?" he asked.

"Six o'clock."

"I'll come by around five-thirty so we can walk over together."

"Sure."

As she wandered off with Laurel, he went back to the bleachers, where Adam was making notes on each of the players.

"We've got impressive new talent this year," he said to Jack. "That Cooper kid, in particular, has some good moves."

He nodded his agreement, proud that his own assessment had been accurate, even more proud because Ava was his. And more than a little annoyed that she was "that Cooper kid" rather than "that Garrett kid."

"About her…"

Adam's gaze didn't shift away from his papers. "Don't worry—I know."

"What do you know?"

"That she's yours."

The teacher did look at him now, and grinned at the surprise Jack didn't doubt was evident on his face.

"There was whispered speculation in the teacher's lounge," Adam confided. "But no confirmation. I was skeptical myself, until I saw her. Then I saw her with a soccer ball, and any lingering doubts vanished."

"It's not public knowledge," Jack told him.

His friend laughed. "You only think it's not."

He scowled at that.

"I do have one question, though," Adam said.

"What's that?"

"You and Kelly Cooper—old news?"

His scowl deepened. "Aren't you dating Melanie Quinlan?"

"Not exclusively."

"And isn't there a rule against dating the parent of a student?"

"She's not my student."

Adam's immediate response proved that he'd already given some thought to the ethical implications. A realization that didn't sit well with Jack.

"You're her coach."

"Only for a few weeks."

Jack didn't bother to respond, because he was confident that before the championship tournament was over, no one would be wondering if he and Kelly were old news.

Kelly's worries about Ava's transition to Parkdale Elementary School had apparently been for naught. Her daughter had settled into the routine of seventh grade with little difficulty. At home, they'd also settled into a routine. After school/work, Ava would do her homework—if she had any—while Kelly got dinner ready. Following the meal, they did dishes together and packed lunches for the next day.

"What did you do at school today?" Kelly asked as she chopped up raw vegetables for their snack.

"We had a pop quiz in math."

"How was it?"

Ava shrugged. "I think I did okay. Then we had a substitute in music who didn't know anything about music, so we watched a movie."

"Glad to know my educational tax dollars aren't being wasted."

"And there's a barbecue at the school on Thursday for Meet the Teacher." She pulled the flyer out of her agenda and set it on the counter.

Kelly glanced up from the cutting board and noted the date. "*This* Thursday? As in *tomorrow?*"

"Yeah." Ava grabbed a stalk of celery, bit into it.

"I'm sorry," Kelly told her. "I have an interdepartmental meeting at six o'clock tomorrow night."

"I thought you weren't going to miss any more of my school stuff because of work. Isn't that why we moved here?"

"One of the reasons," she acknowledged. And maybe she could miss a meeting, but she didn't want to miss *this one* because it was the first since she'd started in her new position at Richmond Pharmaceuticals.

Ava shrugged. "Whatever."

"I'm sorry," she said again.

"S'okay," Ava said around another bite of celery. "My dad said he would go."

Kelly had noticed that Ava always referred to Jackson as "my dad" when she was talking to her, but she never actually used the title in his presence. She didn't know if that was because Ava was insightful enough to realize that Jackson was still a little intimidated by the word, or if she simply wanted to emphasize the relationship Kelly had denied for so long.

"When did you see Jackson?" she asked her daughter.

"He was at my soccer tryout after school."

"You were supposed to go to Laurel's house after school."

"I went to Laurel's house after tryouts," Ava said patiently. "And then her mom brought me home after we'd finished our science project."

"Is Laurel trying out for the team, too?"

"Yeah. We both made the first cut. Next tryout's Friday at lunch. Coach Webber said he'll make the final cuts then."

"Are you worried?"

"Not really. My dad said he'd come by later so that we could work on some stuff." Her eyes lit up in response to the ring of the doorbell. "In fact, that's probably him now."

"Apparently I should have been a lawyer instead of an accountant," Kelly grumbled to herself as her daughter raced to the door.

* * *

Shortly after father and daughter had headed off to the park and Kelly had finished packing lunches, Lukas stopped by to take his "favorite girls" for ice cream.

"Ava's not here," Kelly told him. "She went to the park with Jacks to work on her corner kicks."

He shrugged philosophically. "How about you? Are you in the mood for a double scoop of mint chocolate chip?"

"Isn't ice cream appropriate for any mood?"

"Absolutely," he agreed.

They chatted easily on the way to Walton's. Kelly told him about her new job at Richmond Pharmaceuticals and Lukas filled her in on Einstein's most recent antics. Once they had their ice cream in hand—a double scoop of mint chocolate chip in a waffle cone for Kelly and a caramel pecan brownie sundae for Lukas—they sat side by side on one of the picnic tables outside.

They talked some more about everything and anything, but it wasn't until their ice cream was nearly done that Lukas finally mentioned his brother's name.

"It seems like Jack's been spending a lot of time with Ava these days."

"He has," she agreed, and tried not to sound too unhappy about it.

"Isn't that what you wanted? The reason you came back to Pinehurst?"

"I thought so." But she hadn't thought Jackson would make such an effort. She'd thought he might spend a couple hours a week with his daughter, but in the past two weeks, he'd been there almost every single day. And on the days that he didn't see her, he at least made a point of calling. "But it seems as if he's seen more of Ava recently than I have."

"It's not a competition, Kelly."

"I know," she said. "Or I know it shouldn't be."

"But you're used to being the center of her world, and now you're not," Lukas guessed.

"Now I'm not even in the same orbit. Lately all she talks about is 'my dad.'"

"Having a father is a new and exciting experience. Don't worry, the novelty will wear off."

She smiled, because she knew that was what he wanted, but the truth was that she didn't want the novelty to wear off. She sincerely hoped that Ava would develop a good relationship with her father—she just didn't want to lose her in the process.

"I've got competition now, too," Lukas reminded her. "When it was just an honorary title, I was her only 'uncle.' Now I have to compete with my own brother to be her favorite."

"I never thought about that," she mused. "That would be a tough competition."

"But Ava's known me longer, so I figure that gives me a slight edge."

"On the other hand, Matt has a wife, three kids, and two puppies, and Ava's always wanted to be part of a big family."

"I've got a puppy," he reminded her. "And a cat."

She smiled. "Yeah, that definitely narrows the gap."

"And I've got two tickets to the Black Keys concert Saturday night."

"I don't think Ava's a fan."

"I wasn't going to take Ava."

Her spirits immediately lifted. "You're going to take me?"

"Do you want to go?"

"I absolutely want to go," she assured him. Then reality hit, and her excitement dimmed. "But—"

"Ask Jack to hang out with Ava," Lukas suggested, anticipating her concern.

"It's a Saturday night."

"That is what it says on the tickets," he confirmed.

"He probably already has plans."

"I know you don't want to believe that he's changed, but he has," Lukas told her. "Jack's wild ways with women are very definitely a thing of the past."

Kelly did want to believe it, but she was afraid to. Because if she did believe it, she might fall for him all over again, and she wasn't going to let that happen.

"Okay," she relented. "I'll ask him." Then she bumped his shoulder with her own. "Thanks."

"For the ticket?"

"Well, that," she agreed. "And for being here."

"Always."

It wasn't nearly as unusual as Kelly thought for Jack not to have plans on a Saturday night. And if he did go out, more often than not it was with one or both of his brothers. But since Matt had married Georgia, it was next to impossible to get him out, and since the incident with Luke at Kelly's house, Jack had been maintaining a cautious distance from his younger brother.

So when Kelly asked him if he could hang out with Ava on Saturday night, he had no reason to refuse the request. In fact, he was happy to have extra time with his daughter. But he was curious about where Kelly was going. The possibility that she might have a date—

Well, he just didn't want to consider that possibility. So he was relieved to learn that she was going to a concert with Luke. Or so he thought until she said goodbye and walked out of the house in high heels, snug-fitting jeans, and a sexy little top, and he realized it wasn't relief that he was feeling.

Based on a few offhand comments that she'd made, he didn't think she'd done much dating. No doubt because she'd been so focused on raising their daughter. But Ava was almost a teenager now, and it wouldn't be too long after that when she herself would start dating—or at least wanting to date. Since Jack had no intention of letting that happen until she was at least twenty-one, that wasn't anything more than a distant concern. The idea of Kelly dating, on the other hand, was a more distinct possibility. And one that he didn't like at all.

Ava popped a DVD into the player while he put a bag of popcorn in the microwave.

"I was wondering about something," she said, when the kernels had stopped popping.

"What's that?" He opened the bag and dumped it into a large plastic bowl.

"Am I supposed to call you Jack? Or Dad?"

He'd noticed that she didn't tend to use any form of direct address when she spoke to him and he suspected that she hadn't yet figured out how he fit into her life. Which wasn't really surprising, since he was still struggling to figure that out himself. And while there was a part of him that wanted to be Ava's "Dad," another part feared that he wasn't worthy of the name. Aside from contributing half of her DNA, what had he done to deserve the title?

"There isn't any *supposed to,*" he said. "It's up to you."

She frowned, clearly dissatisfied with his response. "It feels weird to call you Jack."

"And it probably feels just as weird to think about calling me Dad."

"Except that you are my dad."

He could see her dilemma, because his was similar. She

was his daughter, but he had yet to refer to her as such in conversation with anyone other than Kelly.

"But we're both new to this father-and-daughter thing," he pointed out. "It would probably be easier if I'd been there when you cut your teeth or started to walk or learned to talk. Then we might have naturally progressed from 'da-da' to 'daddy' to 'dad'—but even most babies take a year to get to 'da-da.'"

"Are you saying that you want me to wait a year to call you Dad?"

"No, I want you to wait until you're ready, whether that's a month or a year or even longer."

She popped the top of her soda and took a sip while she considered, then nodded. "Okay."

With that matter decided, at least for the moment, they settled down in the living room to watch the movie. As the action played out on the screen, Jack found himself thinking about everything he'd missed over the past twelve years. And when he started counting all those milestones that had passed without him even being aware that he had a child, he couldn't help but feel angry with Kelly.

But being here with Ava now, just hanging out with his daughter on a Saturday night, was a milestone he'd never thought he would experience. And as she yawned and let her head drop onto his shoulder, he realized that he wouldn't trade this night for anything in the world.

When the movie was over, he picked up the empty popcorn bowl and soda cans while she ejected the disc.

"I have one more question," she told him.

He braced himself. "What's that?"

"Can I have a puppy?"

He laughed. "*That's* a question you have to ask your mother."

* * *

Kelly had a fabulous time at the concert, so much so that she actually stopped worrying about Ava and Jackson for a few hours. And she was happy to spend the time with Lukas. She wasn't sure he'd completely forgiven her for keeping the identity of her daughter's father a secret for so long, but she was confident that their friendship was back on track.

As a result, when she got home Saturday night, Kelly felt as if there wasn't anything she couldn't handle. The feeling lasted only until she sat down at the kitchen table with a mug of peppermint tea and Jackson said, "I've been thinking about what Ava said—about wanting to live with me."

Kelly tried to ignore the knots that tightened in her belly as she picked up her mug. "Even if you had a spare room, I wouldn't let her move in with you."

"I know," he admitted. "And I was actually thinking that it makes more sense for me to move in here."

She was shaking her head before he finished speaking.

"Why not?" he demanded.

"There are so many reasons why not, I don't know where to begin."

"I'm Ava's father."

"A status that is independent of your home address."

He scowled. "You could at least pretend to consider it. Or do you hate me so much that you can't stand being in close proximity?"

Kelly wished she could say yes. Unfortunately, her feelings for Jackson had never been that simple. "I don't hate you at all—I just don't want to live with you."

"I want to get to know my daughter. How is that going to happen when I only see her for a few hours a couple of times a week?"

"It will happen," she assured him. "But you've got to give it time."

"We've already waited more than twelve years."

Whether or not the statement was intended to make Kelly feel guilty, it certainly had that effect. It also made her wonder if what he was asking was really so unreasonable.

She was pleased that Jackson wanted more time with Ava, and she knew that their daughter would be thrilled to have more time with her father. But if that time together was under her roof, Kelly couldn't help but worry how that would impact her. It might be selfish, but it was undeniable. There was no way to pretend that she was unaffected by Jackson's presence, and if they were actually living together, as if they were a real family, she feared that she would fall for him all over again.

"I get that you want more time together," she finally said. "But you don't have to move in here...." Her words trailed off when she saw her daughter standing in the doorway.

Ava's sleepy gaze sharpened as it shifted from Kelly to Jackson. "You're going to move in here?"

"No!" Kelly said quickly, firmly. And then, in a more level tone, "I thought you were asleep."

"I was. Then I woke up and heard voices, so I came down."

"And interrupted a private conversation," she admonished.

"About Jack moving in here."

"No one's moving anywhere."

Ava's hopeful smile faded. "Why not?"

"Because..." Kelly looked around for help, but none was forthcoming.

"Please, Mom." Then she turned to Jackson. "Would you want to live with us?"

"I'm willing to give it a try," he said, "if your mother is."

Of course Kelly wasn't willing—and she didn't believe that Jackson wanted to move out of his high-end downtown condo to a house in suburbia with an ex-lover and their twelve-year-old daughter. But he obviously didn't want to disappoint their daughter, so he was going to make her do it.

"Mom?" Ava prompted.

And when Kelly looked at her daughter again, she found that she couldn't. Because she knew that if she refused to let Jackson move in when he'd already said he was willing to do so, Ava would never forgive her. Kelly already felt guilty enough for depriving her daughter of her father for so many years, and she really didn't want to stand in the way of their developing relationship now. She really didn't want to live under the same roof with Jackson, either but how could she worry about protecting her own heart when her daughter's was so vulnerable and needy? And what Ava really needed right now was her father.

"I guess we can give it a try," she finally relented.

Ava rushed over and hugged her. "Thanks, Mom." Then her attention shifted to her father again. "When can you move in?"

"I'll pack some things tomorrow," he promised.

It was a prospect that didn't help Kelly sleep that night. And by the time she'd cleared up breakfast dishes and dropped Ava off at Laurel's house the next day, she'd had second and third thoughts about her decision.

"Please tell me you're not actually packing," Kelly said, when Jack responded to her knock on his door just before noon on Sunday.

"I'm not actually packing," he said obediently.

She exhaled, so visibly relieved he nearly smiled. "I'm glad you came to your senses."

"I didn't know I'd lost them—and I only said that I wasn't packing because that's what you told me to say."

She frowned at that.

"You told Ava that you were willing to give it a shot," he reminded her, stepping away from the door so that she could enter.

She huffed out an exasperated breath as she followed him into the foyer. "Because my back was against the wall. But the more I think about it, the more I know this won't work. It's an impossible situation."

"Actually, it's not just possible but practical."

She shook her head. "I'm asking you to take the lead here and to tell Ava that you've reconsidered."

"But I haven't reconsidered," he said mildly.

"Well, you should. Because the two of us living under the same roof is a bad idea."

He shifted closer, deliberately invading her space. "Afraid you won't be able to withstand the temptation?"

She held her ground and tipped her head back to meet his gaze. "I promise you, Jacks, I'm not the least bit tempted— except maybe to slap you for being such an arrogant ass."

"I don't think you'd be so angry if you didn't still have feelings for me."

"I didn't come here to feed into your delusions but to try to talk you out of this crazy plan. If that's not possible, we need to at least set some ground rules."

Her prim attitude and cool demeanor tempted him to ruffle her feathers, but her statement also piqued his curiosity. "What kind of ground rules?"

She crossed her arms over her chest in a gesture so similar to their daughter's that he nearly smiled. But then he noticed that the movement pushed her breasts together, enhancing his view of the cleavage visible down the V-neckline of her top. He caught a glimpse of the scalloped edging on the cup of her bra, silky peach-colored lace against satiny pale skin. There were five more buttons down the front of her top, round pearl-like buttons that he could have unfastened in about three seconds. Maybe less.

The possibility was tempting…and incredibly arousing. His response to her was baffling, but undeniable. And while he wanted to believe it was purely physical, because sexual attraction was something he understood, he worried that his feelings for her were deeper and more complex than he was willing to acknowledge.

"First, I want a two-week trial, and I want you to tell Ava that we agreed to a two-week trial."

"Three weeks," he countered.

"Fine. Three weeks," she relented. "Second—but most importantly—you're not bringing women to the house."

It took a moment for her words to register, and when they did, he felt as if he'd had a bucket of ice water dumped over his head. He lifted his gaze from the tempting view of her cleavage to her golden eyes. "You're kidding."

"No, I'm not kidding," she snapped. "I don't want a series of your girlfriends in and out of my daughter's life."

"For God's sake, Kelly. I wasn't talking about your so-called rule, but the fact that you actually thought you had to spell it out to me."

"I might have been gone more than a dozen years, but I haven't forgotten your reputation, Jack."

"I'm not the same man I was then."

"I'm sure the blonde in the red dress would beg to differ."

He gritted his teeth. "I told you that she was a client."

"Well, I'd appreciate it if you entertained your 'clients'

away from my home," she said stiffly. And then she continued, almost apologetically, "I'm not trying to interfere with your social life. I'm just asking you to ensure that my daughter isn't a witness to the parade of women through your life."

"*Our* daughter," he reminded her.

"Our daughter," she agreed.

"Can I say something now?"

She eyed him warily. "What's that?"

"Instead of worrying about nonexistent parades of women, you should think about the fact that I haven't wanted any other woman since I saw you at the airport more than four weeks ago." He shifted closer. "But I definitely want you."

Her eyes widened slightly, but she'd never been the type to back down, and she didn't do so now. Instead, she lifted her chin. "No doubt that's because I'm the only woman in town you haven't slept with at least once in the past decade."

As soon as the words were out of her mouth, Kelly wished she could take them back. The intense focus of the gaze Jackson narrowed on her warned that it was already too late. She'd waved the red cape in front of an angry bull. He took a step closer, so close that she could feel the heat emanating from his body, the frustration rising in waves around him.

Yeah, he was angry. But there was something else in the predatory gleam in his eyes, something that looked a lot like arousal. And—heaven help her—his nearness was definitely stirring her up inside.

"It's been a long time," he acknowledged, and though his tone was casual, his gaze was heated, hungry. "But I can still remember how soft your skin felt beneath my hands, how you trembled when I touched you, how you came apart when I was buried deep inside you."

Her knees were trembling now, but she refused to let him know it. She dropped her arms, her hands reaching behind her to grip the edge of the table at her back. "I'm not the same naive girl I was back then."

He dipped his head, so that his lips were close to her ear. "And I'm not the same boy who couldn't think of anything but getting into your pants. What is the same is the desire—I want you just as much as I wanted you back then. Maybe even more."

She knew what he meant. The attraction she'd felt at twenty-one was nothing like the torrent of need raging inside of her now. And when his tongue traced the outer shell of her ear, the slow, sensuous glide turned her bones to jelly and made everything inside her quiver. But she also knew that succumbing to the want that pulsed through her every vein would be a mistake. And she'd already made enough of those where Jackson was concerned.

His breath was warm on her cheek as his teeth tugged gently on her lobe. He'd barely touched her, but her entire body was suddenly hot and achy. She felt tingles in her breasts, between her thighs. She put her hand up, against his chest, and felt his heart thud wildly against her palm. But instead of pushing him away, her fingers curled into the fabric of his shirt.

His lips skimmed across her jaw. "This is why you really came here, isn't it?"

She shook her head. "I came here to *talk*."

"Tell me you don't want me."

She closed her eyes, bit hard on her lip to hold back the moan when his mouth moved down her throat. "I don't want you."

But it was a lie, and they both knew it.

And when his lips touched the frantically beating pulse point below her ear, she shivered.

"I don't *want* to want you," she clarified.

He'd already made quick work of the buttons running down the front of her blouse, and he dipped his head lower, his tongue delving in the hollow between her breasts.

Inside the lacy cups of her bra, her nipples pebbled, aching for his touch. She closed her eyes against the sting of tears. Dammit, she did *not* want this. Because she knew that getting naked with Jackson would be a mistake for so many reasons. But right now, she couldn't think of a single one of those reasons. She couldn't seem to focus on what was smart or reasonable. She couldn't think at all, but she instinctively knew that this was what she needed. *He* was what she needed.

She pulled his head down, nibbled on his bottom lip. He had a fabulous mouth. Lush and tasty, and incredibly talented. And his hands—oh, those hands were moving over her now, teasing and tempting, making her burn everywhere they touched.

She tore her mouth from his to say, "This doesn't change anything, Jacks."

"I'm not trying to change a thing," he assured her, then cupped her buttocks to lift her up against him.

She wrapped her legs around his waist, rubbed herself wantonly against the hard press of his denim as he carted her down the hall. "You have to know this is a bad idea."

"I can't think of a worse one," he agreed, then kicked open the door of his bedroom and tumbled with her onto the bed.

Chapter Ten

He tugged off her blouse and tossed it toward the floor. Kelly yanked his shirt out of his pants and slid her hands beneath the hem. The taut muscles of his abdomen quivered as she ran her palms from his belly to his chest, reveling in the warmth and strength beneath her fingertips.

He straddled her hips and unfastened the center clasp of her bra. As he pushed the lacy cups aside, Kelly felt everything inside of her clench in anticipation. He lowered his head and flicked his tongue over one already taut nipple, then the other, and a low moan sounded deep in her throat.

While his lips nibbled teasingly at her breasts, his hands moved lower. He slid her skirt up and her panties down, and then his hand was between her legs, those clever fingers dipping into the slick folds. This time it was Jackson who groaned, a sound of pure male appreciation. "You're so wet…and ready."

She could only nod as his thumb moved over her most sensitive flesh and everything inside of her began to tighten.

The first time she'd been with Jackson, he'd simply and completely overwhelmed her. He'd instinctively known how and where to touch her, and he'd driven her to distraction with his hands and his lips and his body. No other man's touch had ever affected her the same way. No one else had ever made her want the way she wanted Jackson, and no one else had ever satisfied her so completely.

Now there was no denying that she wanted. And while his fingers continued to work their magic between her thighs, he fastened his mouth over her breast and suckled her nipple, hard. She cried out as fiery spears of desire shot through her system, arrowing toward her center. There was so much sensation, so much pleasure—and still there was more. He continued to touch and taste and tease, until it was finally…too much. And she shattered.

But despite the waves of pleasure that washed over her, she still felt empty, aching for him. "Please…"

"Tell me what you want," he commanded.

"You." She opened her eyes. "I want you, Jacks."

He pulled away only long enough to shed the rest of his clothes. Then he was stretched out on top of her, his naked body against hers, and it felt so gloriously wonderful.

There was still a small part of her rational brain trying to warn that they were approaching the point of no return, but the quiet logic was drowned out by the clamoring demands of her hormones.

He reached into the bedside table for a foil packet and quickly sheathed himself. Then he lifted her hips off of the bed and buried himself inside of her in one hard, deep thrust.

She cried out at the shock—and pleasure—of the invasion, as new waves of sensation began to ripple through her. He began to move, slow and steady at first, giving her a chance to catch her breath. But she didn't want to breathe; she only wanted to feel. She wrapped her legs around him, pulling him deep, deeper, inside.

Her head fell back against the pillow, but she didn't realize she'd closed her eyes again until he said, "Look at me, Kelly."

She didn't want to—she didn't want to experience the intimacy of that visual connection. But in that moment, she couldn't deny him anything he asked. And when she opened her eyes, she found his locked on her.

"You are so...unbelievably...beautiful."

"Jacks..." She didn't know what else to say. This wasn't supposed to be some emotional bonding moment, it was supposed to be sex. Raw and primal and more powerful than anything else she'd ever known.

Thankfully, he didn't seem to expect her to say anything more. Instead, he captured her mouth in a long, slow, deep kiss that made her blood pulse and her heart ache. As the tension built inside of her again, past and present tangled together so that she didn't know which was real. But it didn't matter.

Nothing mattered except that she was in his arms—exactly where she wanted to be. And they plunged into the abyss of pleasure together.

It was absolutely, undeniably the most incredible sexual experience of her life. And he was absolutely, undeniably the last man on the face of the earth that she wanted to share it with.

What was wrong with her that she was still attracted to the man who had once broken her heart into a gazillion jagged little pieces?

She'd dated other men—not a lot, but a few—who were smart and funny and kind. But she'd never felt the same overpowering desire for any one of them that she felt for Jackson Garrett.

No one had ever touched her the way he touched her. No one had ever made her feel the way he made her feel. And no one had broken her heart as carelessly and completely as he'd done. And she wasn't going to let that happen again.

Feigning a nonchalance she wasn't anywhere close to feeling, she pushed herself off of the bed and began to gather her clothes. She'd thought—*hoped*—Jackson was sleeping, but the rustle of sheets as he sat up in bed proved otherwise.

"What are you doing?" His voice was quiet and controlled, but there was just a hint of frustration around the edges.

She didn't—couldn't—look at him. "I'm leaving."

"Sneaking out?" he taunted.

"No, I just have to go."

"Don't you think we should talk about this?"

"No," she said again, and focused on fastening the buttons of her blouse. "I absolutely do *not* want to talk about it."

"What do you want to do—act like it never happened?"

She tugged the hem of her skirt and stepped into her shoes. "It never should have happened."

"It was inevitable." He was out of bed now, too, and tugging on his jeans.

She shook her head. "I don't do things like this."

"I'd say our twelve-year-old daughter is proof to the contrary."

"Correction," she said coolly. "I've done something like this exactly twice in my lifetime."

"And both times with me? I'm flattered."

Her gaze narrowed. "You're a bastard."

"Actually, *my* parents were married." He tugged his shirt on over his head. "Maybe that's something we should consider."

He said it as casually as if he were suggesting a restaurant for dinner. She responded with a blunt and simple, "No."

"Ava told me she's always wanted a real family."

And Kelly had always wished, more than anything, that she could give her daughter what she wanted. But it wasn't going to happen like this. "And I've always wanted to win the lottery."

He shrugged. "It was just a thought."

His casual dismissal was as insulting as his offhand proposal and not even worthy of a reply. She simply stalked out of the room.

It amazed Jack that Kelly always seemed so cool and composed—except in the bedroom. There, she was all fire and passion, eager to give and to take, to please and be pleased. She was his most erotic fantasy and his biggest weakness.

He'd wanted a lot of women, and he'd had a lot of women. But he'd never needed anyone—except for Kelly. And he didn't like the feeling. He wasn't comfortable with the desperate gnawing in his belly. When he was with her, it was as if he needed to touch her more than he needed to breathe.

He was a man who liked to be in control, and he was never in control around Kelly Cooper. That one weekend in Chicago had made the point clear to him, and even when he'd left the city, he hadn't been able to get her out of his mind.

His reconciliation with Sara had been the desperate act of a desperate man, and an unsuccessful one at that. He wasn't going to make the same mistake again. This time, he wasn't going to let Kelly go.

She paused in the hall, probably trying to remember where she'd left her purse. She found it on the table in the foyer, and immediately began fumbling around inside of it. He guessed that she was probably looking for her keys, but she was too flustered to see that they were beside the bag on the table.

"If this was part of your plan to change my mind about

moving in, it didn't work." He picked up the ring of keys that were on the table, dangled them in front of her eyes. When she reached for them, he closed his hand—capturing her hand along with the keys. "If anything, I'm even more committed now. And I'm going to get under your skin the way you've gotten under mine."

"I thought this was about Ava."

"Ava is only part of the whole equation."

"Ava's the only part that matters," she insisted.

He didn't argue. There was no point when he knew she would only give him the cold shoulder and walk out the door. But she wouldn't be able to do that when they were living under the same roof.

"If you're rushing home to get my room ready before moving day, you should know that I only sleep on Egyptian cotton."

"Bring your own damn sheets."

"Language," he chided gently. "You wouldn't talk that way in front of our daughter, would you?"

She tugged the keys out of his grasp, giving him the satisfaction of knowing that she wasn't so cool or reserved right now.

"And I'm going to need a key," he said, his tone mild.

She yanked the door open—and found herself face-to-face with Lukas.

Jack, experiencing an odd and uncomfortable sense of déjà vu, immediately took a step back.

"Well, this is...unexpected," Lukas noted.

"I have to go get Ava," Kelly said to his brother.

Jack waited until she was halfway out the door before he said, "Don't forget about the key."

Her response was an anatomical impossibility that had Luke's eyebrows lifting.

"Do I want to know what you did to warrant such a

reply?" his brother asked when Kelly had stomped off down the hall.

"Probably not." Jack wandered into the kitchen, keeping a safe distance between himself and his brother. He pulled two bottles of beer out of the fridge, offered one to Luke. When it was accepted, their unspoken truce was sealed.

"Any particular reason you stopped by?"

"To drink your beer," Luke said easily.

"Anytime."

"And to find out if the rumors are true. I heard through Matt, because Ava told Georgia, that you're moving in with your daughter and her mother."

"It's true. For a three-week trial period, anyway."

"Whose idea was this?"

"Ava's."

"What does Kelly think of the plan?"

"She wants to do what's best for Ava."

"Is that why she was here?"

Jack sipped his beer. "Can we maybe talk about something that isn't going to make you want to hit me?"

Lukas flexed his fingers. "I'm not going to hit you," he said. "Aside from the fact that your jaw's like a rock and I need my hands for surgery, I'm starting to see that there's more going on here than the simple fact that you knocked up my best friend thirteen years ago."

The words made him more wary than if his brother had clenched his fists. "What are you talking about?"

"You and Kelly. I never saw it way back when, but I realize now that I should have. And I can't help but think that the two of you might have ended up together if I hadn't interfered."

"Nothing that happened was your fault."

"I went to you for advice, because she told me that she was in love and re-evaluating her future plans. She was so close to finishing school, and I was afraid she was thinking about dropping out. I didn't know the guy she'd fallen in love with was you—or that she was pregnant."

"I'd already decided, long before you ever talked to me, that I had to make it clear to Kelly that our relationship wasn't going anywhere."

"Because you didn't love her?" Luke challenged. "Or because you did?"

"Because I was terrified of the way she looked at me, as if I was everything to her."

"And you were afraid you'd disappoint her."

"As I did, in spectacular fashion."

His brother could hardly dispute the point. "So what do you want from her now?"

"Everything," Jack admitted.

"I never could figure out why you became a serial dater after your divorce," Luke said. "I didn't believe it was a side effect of your failed marriage. It wasn't until I saw you and Kelly together that I realized the truth."

"What truth?"

"That you were never able to give your heart to any other woman because you'd already given it to Kelly."

It was a truth that Jack had only recently acknowledged himself. But accepting his feelings for Kelly didn't make it any easier for him to forgive her deception.

"You were in love with her then, and you're still in love with her now," Luke continued.

Jack wasn't sure he was ready to use that particular word, so he only said, "I've never felt about anyone else the way I feel about Kelly."

"They why were you smiling when she walked out of here cursing your very existence?"

"Because it proved that she isn't indifferent to me."

Luke shook his head. "I hope you know what the hell you're doing."

"So do I," Jack admitted.

Kelly fluffed the decorative pillows on the bed and stepped back to survey her handiwork. She'd had more than a few doubts and second thoughts as she'd loaded up her cart at Betty's Boudoir; she'd known her actions were both petty and immature. But she needed to do something, to take back just a little bit of control over a situation that was rapidly spiraling out of her control.

And, in a roundabout way, it *had* been Jackson's idea.

That thought made her smile as she poured the rose-scented potpourri into the glass bowl on the bedside table.

As the estimated time of his arrival drew nearer, the doubts and second thoughts came back with a vengeance. But by that time, it was too late to undo what had already been done. Instead, she kept herself busy in the kitchen, stuffing pork chops for dinner.

Ava had offered to help, so Kelly had put her to work peeling potatoes. The relatively simple task took her daughter almost an hour, because every time she finished peeling one potato, she would wander into the living room to look out the front window, searching for her father's car. It was as if she feared he'd drive right past the house if she wasn't watching for him, and realizing how excited her daughter was about Jackson moving in only made Kelly feel guiltier.

When he finally did arrive, Kelly was almost as relieved as Ava—and more than a little worried that she might have started something she didn't know how to finish.

Jack understood that Kelly had reservations about this arrangement. Hell, he had more than a few of his own. But he wanted to make it work, because it was what Ava wanted. And because it meant that he would get to see a lot more of his daughter and her mother.

He didn't expect that Kelly would have rolled out the red carpet in anticipation of his arrival, and that was okay. Especially when Ava's enthusiastic welcome more than compensated for her mother's lackluster one.

"Is that all you brought?" Ava eyed the garment bag and small suitcase with obvious disappointment.

"I wasn't sure how much room I'd have," he explained. He didn't remind her that this was a trial arrangement and that it was entirely possible—probable even—that he would be moving out again in a few weeks.

"You've got two dressers and a walk-in closet," she told him. "Can I help you unpack?"

"Sure."

She skipped ahead of him down the hall and opened the door.

Jack stood frozen on the threshold. "Maybe I should have asked to see the room before I agreed to this plan."

Ava peeked past him, her eyes widening. "I don't think it looked like this before."

His brows lifted. "How did it look before?"

"The walls were pink," she admitted. "Cuz it was Mrs. Garrett's mom's room when she lived here. And there were pink pillows on the bed, but I thought the comforter was chocolate brown."

He could have lived with chocolate brown with pink accents, especially if it was only for a few weeks. But he could *not* live in this, not even for one night.

Pink didn't begin to describe it. The curtains that draped the wide window were sheer and ruffled and the color of bubblegum, and the ruffled shade on the lamp on the bed-side table was the same color. The bed itself was covered in a spread of fuchsia satin and piled high with ruffled pillows in more shades of pink than he ever could have imagined.

He blinked once, then again. Unfortunately, each time he opened his eyes, the room remained unchanged.

"I can't sleep in this," he said. "I'll have nightmares about satin ruffles."

Ava's smile faded, her gaze dropped. "You're not going to stay?"

"I'm staying," he promised her. No way was he letting Kelly get rid of him that easily. "But I'm going to make a few changes in here."

"What kind of changes?"

"Do you have any boxes left from when you moved?"

"A whole pile in the basement."

"Let's get some of them up here so we can pack up these perfume bottles and doilies." He looked at the pile of pillows on top of the satin spread and shuddered. "We're going to need some garbage bags, too."

As she'd been cooking, Kelly had decided that she would tell Jackson not to expect a meal on the table every night. She might have agreed to let him move in temporarily, but she wasn't going to be his cook or his maid. But he ate with such enthusiasm, complimenting her on the pork chops, garlic mashed potatoes and buttered beans, that she couldn't get the words out. Besides, whether she was cooking for two or for three, she had to cook, and it was a sincere pleasure to feed someone who obviously appreciated her efforts.

Kelly had always enjoyed creating in the kitchen, but in the past year, she'd had little opportunity—and less time— to prepare meals like this, and she and Ava had eaten more takeout than she wanted to admit.

Now that her schedule was more defined, she'd started

looking in her cookbooks again and making grocery lists with specific recipes in mind. Although Ava would be happy with tacos or fajitas or nachos every night of the week, she wasn't really a fussy eater, and Kelly was pleased to be able to offer different and healthier options.

When dinner was finished, Ava cleared the table and Jackson loaded the dishwasher. They worked well together, and as Kelly scrubbed up the pans, she realized it would be far too easy to fall into the rhythms and routines of a family—and far too tempting.

After her duties were done, Ava went upstairs to email Rachel. Jackson finished drying the pans, then said to Kelly, "There was a brown comforter in the dryer that Ava said I could use."

"Sure, if that's what you want," she said agreeably. "I just thought the new one brightened the room."

"I figured it was new, because it still had a price tag on it. So did the pillows and the curtains."

She shrugged. "Just in case they weren't to your taste and I had to take them back."

"The comforter was on sale for seven dollars."

"I thought I should try to be frugal, since you seem so concerned about my financial situation."

"So you were looking in the clearance section, not the ugly section?"

"You don't like ruffles and lace?"

He pinned her with his gaze. "I have no objection to ruffles and lace—especially if you're wearing them. But I'm not sleeping in a room that looks like it was decorated by Barbie on crack."

She felt her lips twitch. "The sheets are Egyptian cotton, as specified."

"The sheets are fine," he agreed. "It was everything else that had to go."

"You put the idea of redecorating in my head—telling me what kind of bedding you wanted."

"Obviously I didn't realize how completely opposed to this arrangement you are."

She shrugged. "I'll deal with it."

"I'm not often accused of being selfless, but I agreed to move in here because it was what Ava wanted and because it's the only thing she's ever asked of me. Well, this and a puppy," he admitted. "But if it's really a problem for you, I can try to make her understand that it just won't work."

"No," Kelly said. "You're right—we should at least give it a try." And then, as if the other part of his comment had only just registered, she looked up at him. "She asked you for a puppy?"

He nodded.

"What did you say?" she asked warily.

"I told her we'd go to the animal shelter after school on Monday."

Her jaw dropped. "You didn't."

"Okay, I didn't," he agreed. "I told her that she'd have to clear that with you."

"Thank you."

"But now I'm thinking that it's not a bad idea."

"Okay." She held up her hands in mock surrender. "I'm sorry about the pink bedding."

Jack seemed to consider her apology, and find it lacking. "I've always been partial to German shepherds."

"*And* the curtains and doilies."

"Although chocolate Labs are beautiful dogs, too," he continued. "Lukas mentioned that he'd be seeing a litter of those soon."

She sighed. "And I'm sorry about the perfume bottles and the potpourri."

"Of course, a dog is a long-term commitment, and not

one that should be undertaken without careful consideration."

"Is that an offer of a truce?"

"Do you cook anything else that tastes as good as those pork chops?" he countered.

"How do medallions of beef tenderloin in a cabernet reduction sound?"

His smile was just a little bit smug. "Sounds like a truce to me."

Chapter Eleven

The revelation that Jack Garrett was the father of Kelly Cooper's daughter barely caused a ripple, but the news that he'd moved in to the house on Larkspur Drive raised more than a few eyebrows. Having grown up in Pinehurst, Kelly should have known better than to think that her private life would remain private, but she still worried about how the gossip and innuendo might affect Ava.

Not that her daughter seemed bothered by any of it. She was too happy to finally have a father—and two uncles, an aunt and three cousins—to worry about anything else. For most of Ava's life, it had just been she and her mom on national holidays and at family events, and she embraced her new extended family with enthusiasm. Kelly just hadn't yet figured out where she fit into the picture.

When the Parkdale Elementary School senior girls' soccer team played in the championship game, the whole Garrett family was in attendance. Although the Panthers lost three to two in the final and Ava was undoubtedly disappointed that her medal said *finalist* rather than *champion,* her mood quickly lifted when Matt and Georgia invited everyone—including her BFF and Laurel's family—back to their place for a barbecue.

After the meal, Kelly helped Georgia with cleanup. It was the first chance they'd had for some one-on-one conversation since Jack had moved in and Kelly wasn't surprised when Georgia asked, "So how's it going, living under the same roof with your sexy and charming ex-lover?"

"It's…awkward."

"I was hoping for something a little juicier than that."

Georgia's unbridled disappointment made Kelly smile.

"Well, I can tell you that we're both trying to make it work. And maybe we're trying too hard. Our conversations are mostly formal and polite—sometimes painfully polite. I find I'm often biting my tongue when Jack says and does things that I know are intended to annoy me because I don't want to fight with him and upset Ava."

"Couples argue—it's a fact of life."

"We're not a couple," Kelly reminded her.

Georgia's brows rose. "You live together, eat meals together, watch TV together and share parenting responsibilities. I don't know what your yardstick is for comparison, but that says 'couple' to me."

"We're not sharing a bed," Kelly pointed out.

"And whose fault is that?" her neighbor challenged. "Because I've seen Jack look at you, and if you're not sleeping together, it's not because he isn't interested."

"It's because I'm more concerned with self-preservation than sexual gratification."

Georgia shook her head. "Silly girl."

Kelly chuckled, but her tone was serious when she said, "I just can't risk it."

"You're afraid to fall in love with him again."

"I'm not afraid, because I'm not going to let it happen."

Her friend's smile was sympathetic. "I wasn't going to let myself fall in love with Matt, either, but it happened. Almost without me even realizing it."

But Kelly shook her head stubbornly. This time her eyes were wide open and her heart was strictly off-limits.

* * *

Jack had spent the better part of the day in court and gotten absolutely nothing accomplished, so he was in a dark mood and not amenable to any new interruptions to his schedule. And then Kelly walked into his office.

"I didn't realize you'd have a waiting room full of clients at this time of day," she said. "I didn't want to bother you, but Colleen assured me you wouldn't mind."

"I don't mind," he said. "But I am curious. The last time you came here, it was to tell me that I had a child."

She smiled, just a little. "No breaking news today. I was just out running some errands and thought I'd check in to see if you wanted to meet Ava and I for dinner after her basketball practice."

"I want to, but I can't. I got caught up in court, so I'm running behind, and I have at least half a dozen clients to see before I can call it a day."

"That's okay. I didn't really expect you would be free."

"I wish I was," he said, sincerely disappointed to have to decline her impromptu invitation. But he took it as a good sign that she'd even issued the invitation. They were into the second week of the three-week trial period that she'd insisted upon for their living arrangement, and she'd finally stopped marking the days off on the calendar. It gave him hope that she wasn't just getting used to having him around but might actually enjoy his presence, rather than simply tolerating it for Ava's sake.

Although his appointments kept him busy for several more hours, he still found his thoughts drifting occasionally. He was confident that he and Ava were on the right track. He and Kelly, on the other hand, seemed to be on very different tracks. She continued to fight the attraction between them, and he didn't want to fight anymore.

When he finally left the office he was tired and hungry—and surprised that Kelly's car wasn't in the driveway. Ava was home, snuggled up in her pajamas and watching TV in her mom's bedroom, and she told him that Kelly had just popped out to pick up a few groceries.

Since there were no leftovers waiting for him tonight, he pulled out some meat and cheese and bread and made himself a sandwich. Kelly came in the back just as he was sitting down at the table.

"I wasn't sure if I'd see you back here tonight," she said.

"Where else would I go?"

She shrugged and started to put the groceries away. "Maybe back to your condo."

As she opened and closed cupboards, he tried to figure out what was going on. Because there was definitely something going on. She'd been in a friendly mood earlier, now she was distant and cool. He bit into his sandwich. "Why would I go there?"

She turned to face him. "Because I saw Miss Scarlet in the waiting room when I was at your office."

Miss Scarlet?

Jack frowned, and then the pieces clicked into place. She was referring to Norah, who liked to dress in red and paint her lips to match.

He pushed his plate aside, his appetite gone. "You really don't think much of me, do you?"

"I don't know what to think when I see a woman like that climbing all over you. Or when I walk into the hardware store and Annalise Wilson makes reference to your intimate history."

"Jesus, Kelly, you know my relationship with Annalise started and ended in high school."

"Not to hear her tell it."

"And you believe her?"

She blew out a weary breath and turned to get a glass

from the cupboard, then filled it from the tap. "No, I don't believe her," she finally said. "But Cassie Silverstone looks at me like she wants to claw my eyes out whenever I see her in the cafeteria at work, because she thinks I'm sleeping with you and she wishes she was, and Leesa Webster looks right through me if our paths cross in town."

"I have no interest in Cassie Silverstone or Leesa Webster," he assured her. "As for the client you saw me with at Mama Leone's—she fired me tonight because I told her I would never sleep with a client."

"She fired you?"

He nodded. "And then she rehired me when I confided that our professional relationship wasn't the only reason I wouldn't sleep with her."

"Aren't you breaching lawyer-client confidentiality by telling me this?"

"I'm not revealing any privileged information," he pointed out. "And I hope you don't mind that I told her I was living with you and not interested in a relationship with anyone but you."

"Do you really think that will dissuade her?"

"I didn't say it to dissuade her. I said it because it's true. I want *you,* Kelly. Only you."

"You only want me because I'm a challenge."

His lips quirked. "I won't deny that you're a challenge."

"It's a game to you," she clarified. "And you've always been intensely competitive. If I said, 'Okay, let's go do it,' that would be the end—game over."

"You want to test that theory?"

She shook her head. "You're here to build a relationship with your daughter," she reminded him.

"Why can't I build a relationship with my daughter's mother at the same time?"

"Because that's not what you really want."

"Don't try to tell me what I want," he said, his voice dangerously soft. "You've been under my skin, and in my heart, for more than thirteen years.

"Did I try to forget about you? Hell, yes. But it didn't work. No other woman was ever able to erase the memory of your warmth, your smile, or your touch. No other woman's kiss satisfied my craving for yours. No other woman felt so right in my arms.

"So don't you dare try to tell me what I want," he said again. "Because you obviously don't have a clue."

Then he dumped the rest of his sandwich in the garbage and shoved his plate in the dishwasher before stalking out of the kitchen.

Kelly stood with her hands still wrapped around her water glass for several minutes after he'd gone. He hadn't touched her, but he'd still managed to leave her shaken to the very core. The stormy intensity in his gaze had made her heart pound and her knees weak. She knew he had a volatile nature, but she'd never seen him like that, and she hadn't known how to respond when every ounce of fury and frustration was focused directly on her.

He'd looked angry. Dangerous. And incredibly hot.

She took a long sip of water to cool herself.

The words—if he hadn't practically shouted them at her—might have warmed her heart. Certainly they suggested that his feelings for her might be stronger than she'd dared to hope.

Her ground rules aside, she hadn't expected Jack to give up his social life, nor did she want him to. Because as long as he was going out with other women, she would remember to keep her guard up. But when he insisted on hanging around the house, spending time with her and Ava, it was harder for Kelly to remember all the reasons she shouldn't fall for him again.

In the absence of those reasons, she would just have to give him a wide berth.

"I have to admit you were right, Jack."

He paused outside of Judge Ryan's courtroom and turned to face Gord Adamson with a grin. "Those words are magic to my ears. But what, exactly, was I right about?"

"Your baseball player."

Travis Hatcher had been granted a conditional discharge pursuant to their joint recommendation of the judge, but he wasn't completely in the clear just yet. He still had twelve months of probation to complete, including an anger management course and fifty hours of community service.

"I appreciate your cooperation, and the vote of confidence," he told his friend.

"I was at the probation office when he came in to sign the papers," Gord said. "Most of the kids that I've met in court would have looked away, even after I've cut them a break. Your guy crosses the room, holds out his hand, *and thanks me.*"

Jack had to smile at the incredulity in his friend's tone.

"And then he says he's going to make sure he stays out of trouble because he wants a baseball scholarship to put him through college so he can maybe be a lawyer someday. Like you."

"Really?" Jack was as pleased as he was surprised by that revelation.

"I told him to set his sights a little higher," Gord said. "Like the ADA's office."

He chuckled. "I'm sure you did."

As he shook Gord's hand, another thought occurred to

him. "Who came in with him to sign the undertaking—his mother or his father?"

The look on his friend's face gave him the answer before he spoke. "Neither. It was his high school baseball coach."

"Damn."

"Some people were not meant to have kids," Gord noted.

Jack just nodded as the ADA walked away. He used to worry that he was one of those people. Actually, that wasn't even true. He'd never worried about it because he'd never given the matter much thought. And because he'd never aspired to parenthood, he'd assumed that he lacked parental instincts.

The past few weeks with Ava had proven otherwise. He didn't think he was going to be a candidate for Father of the Year anytime soon, but he would make sure that his daughter never had cause to doubt how much he loved her.

Jack's experience in family court had demonstrated time and time again how crucial parental involvement was to a child's success in life. And he realized that the abandonment by Kelly's parents was probably one of the reasons she was so wary about rekindling their relationship. She didn't trust him to stand by her, and why should she? He'd left her once already, after she'd been abandoned by her mother and her father—the two people who should have loved her most. And then her husband had walked out, too, choosing the advancement of his career over his marriage.

He knew it would be an uphill battle, but he was going to prove to Kelly that not only could he stick, he wanted to.

On Wednesday, Jack had a meeting at Legal Aid after work, so it was just Kelly and Ava at the dinner table.

"Did you finish all of your homework?" Kelly asked.

"Except for social studies." Ava made a face as she pushed a piece of cauliflower around her plate. She disliked social studies as much as she disliked cauliflower. "I'm supposed to research European colonization of the Americas."

"That's a pretty hefty subject."

"It's a group project that Mrs. Kellner wants us to work on at the library. She said she wants proper research, not just an internet search."

"Who are you working with?"

"Laurel and Hayley. They want to meet at the library tonight at six o'clock, if that's okay."

Kelly glanced at the clock, saw that it was almost quarter to six already. "You're trying to get out of kitchen duty again, aren't you?"

"Actually, if I had a choice between dirty dishes and history, I'd probably choose the dishes."

"Well, tonight you get a reprieve," she told her daughter. "Go wash up and get your stuff together. I'll drop you off at the library and give you my cell phone so that you can call home for a ride when you're finished."

When the phone rang at eight o'clock, Kelly assumed it would be Ava calling, but it was Jack to say that he was on his way home. Since the library was en route, she asked him to pick up Ava; then she called their daughter and relayed the plan.

Half an hour later, the back door slammed.

Kelly looked up from the book she was reading as Ava stormed through the living room. "How did your research go?"

"I hate him!"

And with that, Ava raced up the stairs and into her bedroom, slamming that door, too.

Kelly set her book aside and followed her path. She tapped on the closed door, then turned the knob. Seeing her daughter in such obvious distress—face down and sobbing into her pillow—made Kelly's heart ache. She cautiously lowered herself on to the edge of the bed and rubbed Ava's back. "Who do you hate?"

"Jack."

The fact that Ava had said "Jack" and not "Dad" warned Kelly of the need to tread carefully even more than the slamming of the doors had done. "What did he do?"

Ava lifted her tear-streaked face. "He told Devin Nicholls that I was in seventh grade."

"I don't know who Devin Nicholls is," Kelly admitted. "But since you are in seventh grade, I'm not seeing the issue."

"Devin's a guy I saw at the high school last week, when we had our class trip to hear the band. He was at the library tonight, and we got talking. He's really cute and smart, and he thought I was in high school."

Kelly mulled over the details for a minute, giving her mind a chance to catch up. She wasn't really surprised that her baby girl was noticing boys—by the time she was twelve, she'd been more than halfway in love with Jackson—but she wasn't ready for those boys to be noticing her back. Especially not high school boys. She pushed aside the unease that stirred inside her and casually asked, "And what were you and Devin doing in the library?"

"Nothing."

She exhaled a slow, unsteady breath.

"Jack *totally* overreacted."

"But what was he reacting to?" Kelly prompted.

"Nothing," she said again. Then she swiped her hands over her tearstained cheeks. "We were upstairs, in the stacks, just talking. And then Devin…well, he kissed me. Sort of."

"He sort of kissed you?"

"His lips *barely* touched mine, then Jack barged in."

"And what did he do?"

"He yelled. In the library." Fresh tears filled her eyes, spilled over. Then she demonstrated. "'Get away from my daughter.' And Devin jumped about ten feet away from me.

"Then he said, 'Let's go, Ava. *Seventh grade* starts early in the morning.'" She buried her face in the pillow again. "He ruined my life."

Kelly winced in sympathy. "I'm sure that wasn't his intention."

"It was the result," Ava responded into the pillow.

Jackson was staring out the kitchen window into the darkness when Kelly came back downstairs.

"Do you want to tell me your side of the story now?"

"She was with a boy in the nonfiction section."

"The nonfiction section?" she said in mock horror.

His gaze narrowed. "Nonfiction is on the upper level. The only time anyone ever goes up there is for privacy."

"Definitely not for research."

"I might not know much about being a father," he admitted. "But I was a fifteen-year-old boy once. If I wanted to be alone with a girl, I would lead her into the nonfiction section, so I know damn well what that kid was thinking."

"And it probably wasn't much different than what she was thinking," she warned him.

He scowled at that. "She's twelve."

"You think only fifteen-year-old boys are ruled by their hormones?"

"Are you saying that I should have left her there with him?"

"No," Kelly said immediately. "I just think you might have handled the situation a little differently."

"She hates me, doesn't she?"

"Let's just say you're not her favorite person at the moment," she told him.

"I saw him lean toward her, and all I could think was, 'Get away from my daughter.' I don't know that I've ever thought of her so clearly and unequivocally as mine to protect."

She smiled. "If you learn not to overreact, you might get the hang of this parenting thing, after all."

"It's scary," he admitted. "Accepting the responsibility, knowing that there will be consequences if I fail."

"There's no pass or fail—it's a learning experience for all of us. And we're all going to make some missteps along the way."

"She reminds me so much of you at that age."

"How would you know?" she challenged. "You didn't pay any attention to me when I was twelve."

"Probably not," he agreed. "But by the time you were sixteen, you scared the hell out of me."

She remembered, all too clearly, how shy and inexperienced she'd been at sixteen, and she couldn't imagine why he would have been afraid. "Why?"

"Because you had no one to look after you." He smiled. "Aside from Lukas, of course."

"Why did I need someone to look out for me?"

"Because you were curious. And I was afraid that if I'd pushed, you wouldn't have pushed me away."

She felt her cheeks flush, because she knew it was true. "Then why did you kiss me?"

"Because I couldn't stop myself. Then you got mad at me."

"I wasn't mad because you kissed me," she told him. "I was mad because you *stopped* kissing me."

"You were sixteen," he said again.

"I knew what I wanted."

"So did I, but I knew that if I let things go any further that night, Lukas would have killed me."

"As if I would have run straight to your brother."

"I wasn't willing to take the chance."

"You didn't worry that I'd tell him we spent the weekend together in Chicago?"

"When I saw you behind the bar at the pub, I couldn't think about anything but how much I wanted you," he admitted.

"The chemistry between us was pretty explosive," she agreed.

"I was never very good at chemistry," he said. "But one of the few things I remember from high school science class is that whatever effect was generated—a bright flash of light or a bubbling liquid—it eventually fizzled out."

"I'm not sure I see your point."

"We never fizzled," he noted. "Which leads me to believe that what's between us is more than simple chemistry."

"Maybe it is," she acknowledged. "But there's too much at stake to play around with it this time."

"Don't use Ava as an excuse. We both care too much about her to let our personal relationship affect her."

"We don't have a personal relationship."

"We have a child together," he reminded her. "I'd say that proves we have a relationship."

"No, that only proves we had sex."

"Great sex."

She blew out a breath. "The details are irrelevant."

"The details keep me up at night—thinking about you, wanting you."

"You're a man," she said dismissively. "Men are always thinking about sex."

"Are you trying to annoy me?" Though his tone was mild, the heat in his gaze was not.

She swallowed. "No."

"You always did know how to push my buttons," he admitted. "And maybe that's what you're doing—trying to push me to make the next move so that you don't have to acknowledge your own feelings. Your own desires."

"Your next move is to talk to your daughter," she told him.

It wasn't quite the direction that Jack wanted to go with their conversation, but he knew Kelly was right.

"Do you want to come up with me?" he asked hopefully.

She shook her head. "You need to do this. She needs to know that she matters enough for you to make the effort."

Because she did, he trudged up the stairs.

"I'm sorry if you think I overreacted," he said, standing in the doorway of Ava's room.

"You *did* overreact."

"I'm just trying to look out for you."

"Why?" she challenged.

Since it was obvious that an invitation wasn't forthcoming, he stopped waiting for one and moved into the room. "Because I'm your father."

"That's just biology."

He settled himself onto the edge of her mattress. "It started with biology," he admitted.

"And then what?" Her tone was derisive. "A parent-teacher barbecue and a few soccer practices somehow developed your nurturing instincts?"

"Don't forget The Fun Warehouse."

She didn't crack a smile.

"Yes, Ava, through those events, I started to get to know you. And the more I learned about you, the more I realized that you are a bright, beautiful young woman. You're caring, compassionate, and more than a little competitive. You've got a soft heart, but you don't like anyone to see your vulnerabilities." He smiled. "You really are more like your mother than either of you probably realizes."

She seemed unimpressed by his analysis. "Do *you* realize I'm almost thirteen?"

"Not until February twelfth."

Ava pouted, obviously not expecting him to know that.

"And even if you were thirteen," he continued. "I still wouldn't have let you sneak off with a fifteen-year-old boy. If you want to hang out with someone—friend, boyfriend, whatever—you should invite him over so that your mom and I can meet him."

"Yeah, cuz that wouldn't be embarrassing," she muttered.

"Probably less embarrassing than me hauling you out of the nonfiction section of the library."

"Maybe," she acknowledged.

"Do we have an understanding?"

She nodded slowly. "But I'm still mad at you."

"I hope, when you get over being mad, that you'll realize I'm setting boundaries because I love you and want you to be smart and safe."

He hadn't practiced a speech. He hadn't known what he was going to say until the words spilled out of his mouth. And though they were probably no different from the words spoken by countless fathers before, they were undeniably true.

When Kelly had first told him that he had a daughter—after the initial shock had faded and the instinctive panic had receded—he'd been curious. As they'd gotten to know one another and slowly overcome their mutual wariness, he'd realized that he genuinely liked her. And then somehow, sometime between that first disastrous dinner and tonight, she'd moved in and taken up permanent residence in his heart. Just like her mother.

Ava blinked damp eyes. "You…love…me?"

"I guess I haven't said that before?"

She shook her head.

"I'm still kind of new at this father thing," he reminded her. "But I do love you."

She sniffled, and though he knew she wasn't yet close to forgiving him, he didn't think she was quite as mad anymore. "There's something Mom used to say to me when I was little, if I was misbehaving."

"I can't believe you ever misbehaved," he said, and earned a small smile.

"Not often," she promised. "But she used to say that she might not like how I was acting, but she always loved me. So I thought I should tell you—I didn't like what you did tonight, but I—I love you, too."

He leaned over to touch his lips to her forehead. "That works for me."

Chapter Twelve

The Pinehurst Fall Festival had been one of Kelly's favorite community events when she was a kid, but not for any of the usual reasons. As much as she'd always enjoyed the rides and the games and the cotton candy, it was the electric buzz of excitement that ran through the crowd that had made the biggest impression on her.

She was curious to know if it would still feel the same or if, as an adult, she would realize that it was the innocence and wonder of youth that had made the event seem much bigger and better than it was. Since she was taking Ava and Laurel, she hoped that they would experience some of the same joy and excitement.

She had planned to be gone before Jackson got home from work. Not that she was avoiding him, exactly. She just found that if she kept some physical distance between them, it was easier to think clearly and remember all the reasons she needed to keep that physical distance between them.

Of course, Jackson seemed to take advantage of every opportunity to invade her personal space and take pleasure in doing so. He liked to touch her, although not in a blatantly sexual way. Just casual, seemingly innocent touches that nevertheless stirred up everything inside her. The briefest stroke made her remember leisurely, lingering caresses; the softest touch inspired memories of hard, impatient demands; the slightest brush of skin made her crave full-body contact.

He was, slowly and relentlessly, seducing her. And Kelly feared that she wouldn't be able to resist him for much longer. And then what? What was his plan? Was it all about the conquest? Or did he want something more?

Until she knew the answers to those questions, maintaining that physical distance wasn't just smart but necessary.

But once again, Jackson thwarted her plans, coming in the back door just as Kelly was spooning leftover rice and stir-fry into a container.

"Dinner," she told him. "If you're hungry."

"You ate early tonight."

She nodded. "I promised to take Ava and Laurel to the fair, and they wanted to get there as soon as possible."

"I almost forgot the fair was this weekend," he said. "Can I tag along?"

She eyed him warily. "It's a Friday night, Jackson. Don't you have a date?"

"You know there's only one woman I want to go out with—" he lifted his hand and skimmed his knuckles gently down her cheek "—and she keeps turning me down."

She swatted his hand away, refusing to let herself be charmed by his easy smile. "Save your charm for someone who's interested."

"You're interested, but you're scared."

"You don't scare me."

"So why won't you go out with me?"

"Because I already have plans," she reminded him.

"I'm just asking to tag along."

"If I let you tag along, it's not a date."

"What is it?"

"It's me letting you tag along."

"What if I buy you cotton candy?" he asked hopefully.

"Still not a date," she said firmly.

"What if I take you on the Ferris wheel?"

Kelly shook her head. "I hate the Ferris wheel."

"Really?"

She glanced away, embarrassed to have admitted to such a weakness. "I'm not fond of heights."

"What if I put my arm around you and held you close?" He slid an arm over her shoulders to demonstrate.

She shook her head. "I don't think that would help."

In fact, she suspected that being in close proximity to Jackson would have the opposite effect. And she knew that she was more willing to risk a turn around the giant wheel than spend thirty seconds in his arms. Because as afraid as she was of high places, she was even more afraid of her growing feelings for Jackson.

"I just want to go to the fair with you," he said, when she remained silent.

"Then you better go get changed. We're supposed to pick Laurel up in half an hour and I doubt you want to traipse through the barn in a designer suit."

"I don't traipse anywhere," he said indignantly.

She glanced at her watch. "Twenty-nine minutes."

He headed for the stairs, already loosening his tie.

Jack did buy her cotton candy, and a glass of cold-pressed apple cider. And he indulged the girls' every wish and whim, buying them tickets for the Zipper, the Ferris wheel, the Tidal Wave, and the Tempest—and then more tickets so they could ride them all again. While Ava and Laurel conquered the midway rides, Jack and Kelly wandered through the barn to check out the livestock exhibits and agricultural displays.

Jackson seemed to know almost everyone in Pinehurst, and every time they turned a corner, they were bumping into someone else who wanted to say hello.

He'd always been popular, but she realized now that

he was also respected and well-liked. As a teenager, he'd earned a reputation for being arrogant, talented and capricious. Now it seemed that he was knowledgeable, successful and steadfast, and Kelly wasn't sure what to think of the apparent changes.

He introduced her to Gord Adamson, a colleague who was at the fair with his wife and their two kids, Pete, his mechanic, and Reginald, a security guard at the courthouse. But it was an exchange with Mrs. Cammalleri that really opened Kelly's eyes.

Kelly had paused to peruse the assortment of fudge for sale when the elderly woman behind the table called out to Jackson. He obediently responded to the summons, and she pulled his head down to kiss both of his cheeks before she asked, "What kind of fudge do you want?"

He looked at Kelly. "What's your favorite?"

"Rocky Road."

The old woman eyed Kelly appraisingly. "She's with you?"

He nodded. "Yeah, this is Kelly. Kelly—Mrs. Cammalleri."

Mrs. Cammalleri smiled at Kelly and rattled off a bunch of Italian as she cut a thick slice of Rocky Road fudge and wrapped it in plastic. Then she added an equally thick slice of Peanut Butter Cup, no doubt because she knew that was Jackson's favorite. Her hands were wrinkled and spotted, but their movements were steady and sure. She put both pieces of fudge in a paper bag and passed it across the table to him. He gave it to Kelly and reached for his wallet.

Mrs. Cammalleri shook her head. "A gift," she said. "Because you're a good man, Jackson Garrett."

He looked around, as if afraid that someone might overhear. "Don't be spreading rumors like that, Mrs. C," he chided.

She chuckled and swatted at him playfully. "He was a bad boy, but he's a good man," she said to Kelly now. "A good man needs a good woman. A family."

"I'm working on that, Mrs. C," Jackson told her.

But the old woman stayed focused on Kelly. "Don't make him work too hard," she advised.

Kelly left the table with the bag of fudge in hand, feeling a little baffled and a lot confused by the brief exchange.

"Are you going to tell me what that was about?" she asked Jackson.

He seemed almost as embarrassed by her quietly spoken question as he'd been by the older woman's exuberant greeting.

"She had a little bit of a legal problem a couple of years back."

"What kind of problem?"

"I can't share the details—lawyer-client confidentiality."

"I bet Mrs. C would be happy to tell me."

He sighed. "It was just a small claims thing."

"I didn't know you did small claims."

"It's not a big part of my practice, but every once in a while, there's a case that piques my interest."

She had a sneaking suspicion that she knew why he was being deliberately vague with the details. "You do *pro bono* work."

He shrugged. "I originally signed up because it sounded like a sexual thing."

But she knew his easy response was a cover. He'd frequently joked that he got into the practice of law because he wanted to make as much money as his brother without the hassle of being summoned to the hospital at all hours. But just last week, she'd woken up in the night and found him pounding away on the keyboard of his laptop at 3:00 a.m. Apparently he'd gotten a call from a client whose estranged spouse had refused to bring the kids home, so he'd been preparing the necessary documentation for an emergency motion the next morning.

"You are a good man, Jackson Garrett," she said, echoing Mrs. Cammalleri's words.

He scowled. "Give me some of that fudge."

They nibbled on the sweet concoction as they wandered through the tables set up to display the wares of the arts and crafts vendors, and they got back to the midway in time to see that Ava and Laurel were joining the Ferris wheel line for the third time.

"I think they would go all night if we let them."

"I have nowhere else that I need to be," Jack assured her.

"I promised Laurel's parents that I would have her home by midnight."

"Then we'll make sure she's home by midnight," he agreed.

"She's a good kid."

"What's the basis for your assessment—the fact that she doesn't have piercings or tattoos?"

"That's a factor," she admitted.

"Newsflash—she has holes in her ears."

Kelly rolled her eyes. "Notwithstanding that fact, I'm glad Ava found her."

"Sometimes we luck out with the people we meet in life," he said, putting his hands on her hips and drawing her closer.

She didn't resist, at least not too much, but her eyes were wide and wary.

"What are you afraid of?" he asked gently.

This time she didn't deny that she was. "I'm afraid that we're both trying to make this into something it isn't."

"I think we both know that it's something," he said, and touched his mouth to hers.

She stayed perfectly still, not leaning in but not pulling away, either. So he kissed her again, softly, slowly, thoroughly, determined to savor the moment. Her lips were warm and soft and sweetly responsive.

He tasted the fudge she'd been eating—dark and rich and temptingly sinful. His hand skimmed up her back, his fingers tangling in the ends of her long, silky tresses, dragging her head back to deepen the kiss. Her tongue touched his, tentatively at first, then again, more boldly.

Desire pulsed through his veins, roared in his blood, drowning out the sounds of the crowd all around them. There was something about kissing Kelly that had always felt so incredibly intimate. As if there was a connection not just between their lips but their souls.

A connection that was violently severed by a three-foot whirling dervish wielding a candy apple like a sword.

Their teeth bumped, their foreheads collided.

"I'm so sorry." The apology was tossed over her shoulder as the child's mother continued her harried pursuit.

Jack swore; Kelly giggled.

He wrapped his arm around her waist and drew her close again, but he only touched his lips to her forehead this time.

"You're driving me crazy," he warned her.

"You know it goes both ways."

"I didn't know." His lips curved. "But I was hoping."

"We have to get Laurel home," she reminded him.

"Sooner or later, we're going to finish this."

She could only nod.

"And my vote's for sooner rather than later," he said.

"I'll take that into consideration."

* * *

When Georgia came to the door in response to Jack's knock, she had a baby in her arms and two puppies at her feet.

"Since when do you knock?" she said, in lieu of a greeting.

He kissed her cheek. "Since my brother doesn't live alone anymore."

"Afraid I might be walking around in the buff or something?" she teased, stepping away from the door so that he could enter.

"Or something." He bent down to pat Finn and Fred so they would stop trying to climb up his legs for attention. "Where's Matt?"

"At the hospital. But he should be home soon."

"That's okay—I wanted to talk to you, if you've got a few minutes."

"I would love some adult conversation," she assured him.

He held up the two bags in his hand. "I brought the boys some kettle corn from the fair."

"They'll be ecstatic," she said. "If there's any left when they get back."

He followed her into the kitchen and put the bags on the counter. "Where are they?"

"Birthday party." She glanced at the clock. "I have almost two hours before they come home to bounce off the walls because they're pumped up on cake and ice cream."

"I won't stay that long," he promised.

"Do you want me to put on some coffee?"

"No, thanks." He was surprised, and pleased, when Pippa held out her arms to him. "Can I?"

"Are you kidding?" Georgia willingly shifted the baby to him.

"Aren't you a pretty girl?" he said, lifting Pippa over his head and earning a beaming smile.

"And aren't you the charmer?"

Jack just grinned. "She looks more and more like her mama every day."

"Do you think so?"

"Absolutely. Matt's going to have to beat off the boys with a stick by the time she starts kindergarten."

"Or duel with them in the stacks of the library."

Jack winced. "Heard about that, did you?"

She nodded. "Yeah, I heard about that."

"It's not easy, trying to be a parent to a twelve-year-old that I didn't even know existed until a few weeks ago."

"I'm sure it's not," she agreed.

Pippa let her head fall onto his shoulder, rubbed her cheek against his shirt. He felt the tug of so many emotions inside his chest: warmth, pleasure, regret. "I missed this part with Ava."

"You missed a lot of parts," Georgia agreed. "Dirty diapers, midnight feedings, projectile vomiting."

"I never thought I wanted to experience any of those things, but now that I know I've missed them, I can't help but feel ripped off."

"I can understand that."

"I know Kelly and I both made mistakes," he admitted. "I don't know if we can get past them."

"Do you want to get past them?" she asked gently.

"*I* do."

"Then I'd say that nothing that happened before matters as much as what you do going forward from now."

He nodded.

"Have you and Lukas resolved things between you?" she asked cautiously.

"Sort of."

"What does that mean?"

"It means that he's decided to forgive me for knocking up his best friend because he's convinced himself that I've been in love with Kelly for thirteen years."

"Is he right?"

"Yeah, but no way am I going to admit that to him."

After spending a long and mostly sleepless night alone in her bed, Kelly awoke feeling edgy and uneasy. The edgy was Jackson's fault. All it had taken was one kiss to get her all stirred up and aching for him. The uneasy was in direct connection to him, too, because she suspected that she might have judged him unfairly.

She thought she knew who he was. True, her opinion had been broadly based on his sketchy reputation layered over her own residual hurt and anger, but she'd had no reason to question that opinion. Not until last night. Now, suddenly, she was starting to question everything she'd ever believed about him.

Since no one knew him better than his brothers, Kelly found herself at Lukas's door. And found Lukas occupied with a pair of unbelievably tiny kittens.

"Someone left them in a shoebox outside the clinic early yesterday morning." He carefully transferred one of the babies to her.

"How old are they?"

"Probably not much more than four weeks, if that."

"Are they going to survive?"

"If I have anything to say about it."

Which was, of course, no less than she expected. Lukas was a dedicated veterinarian who went above and beyond and who, even after more than a decade at his practice, still took it to heart whenever he couldn't save an animal.

"Have you named them?"

"This one's Boots," he said, pointing to the white feet that made the kitten look as if it were wearing boots. "And that one's Puss."

"Puss and Boots," she realized, and smiled.

"So what's got you in a mood?" he asked.

"I'm not in a mood," she denied.

"That furrow between your brows says otherwise."

She sighed. "I'm confused," she admitted, gently stroking the soft fur of the kitten that was tucked in the crook of her arm. "I'm generally a pretty good judge of character and I hate when people turn out to be different than I expected."

"Different—how?"

She huffed out a breath. "He wasn't supposed to have depth."

"Am I supposed to know what you're talking about?" Lukas asked.

"Jackson." She said his name as if it was a curse.

Lukas feigned shock. "He has depth?"

She glared at him. "Apparently."

Her friend chuckled. "What did he do?"

"I don't know exactly," she admitted. "I just know that it was a *pro bono* case in small claims court for Mrs. Cammalleri."

"He took on the contractor who did her roof," he explained. "Shortly after she paid for the repair, Mrs. C went to Syracuse to stay with her daughter, who had just had a baby. While she was away, we had a huge storm and, for three days, water leaked through the roof—around the chimney where the guy forgot to install new flashing—and into her kitchen, severely damaging her upper cabinets."

"The roofer was obviously negligent."

"Obviously," Luke agreed. "But the insurance company wanted to replace the cabinets with a similar—but much more economical—style from the local DIY store, and Mrs. C wanted them professionally stripped, sanded and refinished, which would be much more labor intensive and, therefore, more costly."

"I would think most people would be happy with a new kitchen," Kelly remarked.

"Most people would. But Mrs. C's husband, now deceased, was a cabinetmaker, and he had made them. The insurance company tried to argue that forty-year-old cabinets weren't worth restoring, but it was the sentimental value that mattered to Mrs. C. So Jack took the case to court for her and got the cabinets restored."

"How do you know all of this?"

"Mrs. C has three cats. While she was going through all of this, one of them—Milo—had a bad upper respiratory infection, so she was making frequent visits to the office." He frowned. "That had to have been four years ago at least."

"Well, she hasn't forgotten. She kissed both of Jackson's cheeks and gave him fudge."

Lukas smiled. "She makes really good fudge."

Kelly wasn't thinking about Mrs. Cammalleri's fudge but about Jackson, and she frowned. "And then, when I finally manage to pry the tiniest details out of him, he acts like it's no big deal."

"Because it wasn't to him," he explained. "It's just what he does."

"I thought he just sat behind his glossy desk overbilling heartbroken clients and splitting up matrimonial assets."

"He does that, too," Luke agreed.

"But he cultivates that image," she grumbled. "As if he

wants people to think he's a morally corrupt and heartless shark who finds pleasure, or at least a paycheck, in the pain of others."

"You can't tell me that any of this really surprises you," Luke said. "If you didn't see past the facade, you would never have fallen for him so completely."

"I was young and inexperienced," she reminded him.

"Maybe you were, when you first fell in love with him," he acknowledged. "But you're not quite as young or inexperienced now, and you're still in love with him."

She wanted to deny it, but they'd both know she was lying. She blew out a breath. "I thought I was at least smarter now. Apparently I'm not that, either."

"So why don't the two of you stop pretending that you're tolerating one another and admit how you feel? Then you could get married and give your daughter the family she's always wanted?"

"For a man who's never taken the matrimonial plunge himself, you're awfully quick to recommend it."

"Because I can see that you guys are meant to be together."

"Except that Jackson has never aspired to be any woman's Mr. Right—he was always focused on being 'Mr. Right Now'—and I have no intention of getting involved with another man who can't stick."

"You thought he was shallow, and you were wrong about that," Lukas pointed out to her. "Maybe you should consider that you might be wrong about this, too."

Chapter Thirteen

Kelly was up to her elbows making Swedish meatballs on Sunday morning when Ava told her that she needed supplies for an art project that was due on Monday, so Jack volunteered to take her to the craft store at the mall. It was supposed to be a quick trip to pick up a few things, but since it was almost lunchtime, Ava suggested that they grab a bite to eat. The food court was never his first choice for a meal, but he was still feeling a little bit guilty about the way he'd handled the library incident so he relented. After he'd finished his pad Thai and she'd polished off her tacos, Ava went to the bathroom to wash up.

He glanced at his watch, noting that she'd been gone for twelve minutes. During that time, several other women had gone in and out, but there was still no sign of Ava.

He hadn't moved from their table, and he didn't think she would have been able to leave without him seeing her go past. But he had taken out his phone to check his email, and he'd taken a few minutes to respond to some of those messages. It was possible that she'd snuck past him while his attention was diverted. But why would she?

Because she was still upset with him for what happened at the library. It was the obvious explanation, but he didn't think it was the right one. Ava wasn't the subtle type—if she was upset with him, she would let him know it. She wouldn't hit back at him by sneaking away and making him worry.

Of course another possibility was that her request for art supplies was just an excuse to get to the mall so that she could meet up with someone else. Maybe even the boy from the library. Or maybe someone she'd met online. He felt a trickle of sweat snake down his back. She was smart and pretty savvy, but she was only twelve. And there were a lot of weirdos and sexual predators in the world.

He glanced at his watch again.

Fourteen minutes now.

He couldn't panic—he needed to keep a clear head and figure out a plan of action. His first instinct was to call Kelly, but he didn't dare. If he was panicking, he could only imagine how she would respond to the news that he'd lost their child.

Except that he had no reason to believe that she was lost. It was entirely possible that she had gone into the washroom as she'd said and simply hadn't come out yet.

He pushed open the door, but kept his body outside. "Ava?"

The only response was a soft, almost inaudible "Go away."

The wave of relief that washed over him was so powerful it nearly knocked him off of his feet. While he still had no idea what might have happened to turn a simple hand-washing exercise into some preteen melodrama, at least he knew she hadn't been abducted.

"I'm not going anywhere without you," he said, pleased that his voice sounded calm and rational. "So hurry up and—"

"I can't."

He frowned. "Ava—"

"Can you—"

Her voice broke, and he realized—somewhat belatedly—that she was crying. Damn. He'd been prepared for a trip to the mall, not an emotional breakdown in a public bathroom.

"Can you call my mom?"

Sure, he could call Kelly, and there was a part of him that wanted to. But if he did, it would be like announcing that he was a failure as a father because he couldn't handle whatever had happened to upset his daughter. And Jack didn't like to fail.

There was a cleaning cart outside, complete with sign "Washroom Temporarily Closed." He stuck the sign in front of the door and went in.

"Go away," she said again.

"Ava, please just tell me what's going on."

"You don't want to know," she said miserably.

"I need to know," he said. "I can't help you if I don't know what's wrong."

She sniffled again. "I got…my…period."

Jack sank down onto the sofa in the living room. "Well, that was an experience I never want to repeat again."

Kelly's lips curved, just a little at the corners, as she handed him a beer. "I figured you needed something a little stronger than coffee after the day that you had."

"You figured right." He tipped the bottle to his lips and drank deeply. Despite his determination to handle Ava's crisis on his own, the four words that she'd spoken through the closed bathroom door had him immediately reaching for his cell phone to call in reinforcements. Kelly had been there in less than fifteen minutes, and he had willingly—in fact, *eagerly*—let her take over. "How's she doing?"

"She's okay. I gave her a heating pad to help ease the cramps and put on one of her favorite movies." She sat down on the other end of the sofa, as far away from Jack as possible. "I guess I'm just surprised that you're still here. I half-expected that you would have dropped her at the door and gone running for the hills."

"There aren't many hills in Pinehurst."

She smiled. "You know what I mean."

"And you should know that I don't bail, Kelly. Maybe I wasn't prepared for what happened today, but nothing is going to make me walk away from Ava." *Or you.* But of course he kept that part to himself because he knew she wasn't ready to believe it.

"I think maybe I underestimated you."

"Maybe?"

"Probably," she allowed. "That wasn't a situation any dad would find easy to deal with, and you handled it well."

He shifted closer and reached for her hand, linked their fingers together. She glanced at him warily, but she didn't pull away. "I know I disappointed you. I'm not going to disappoint our daughter."

"I know you won't. You're a good dad, Jackson."

Her simple and sincere statement warmed his heart as no effusive words of praise had ever done.

"It's easy when you've got a good kid to work with," he noted. "So I guess I should thank you for that."

"Does that mean you've forgiven me for keeping Ava's existence a secret for so long?"

"It means I'm more grateful than angry now, because I've realized that although I missed the first twelve years of her life, I have a chance to know her now." He squeezed her hand gently. "But if you're feeling guilty, there is one thing you could do to help assuage your guilt."

"We both made mistakes," she reminded him. "Why am I the only one who's feeling guilty?"

"I'm a lawyer—my moral compass isn't as strict as yours."

"There was a time when I might have believed that," she told him. "I don't anymore."

"Then maybe you won't object to what I'm going to ask."

"You want to change her name," she guessed.

"Not the Ava part," he assured her.

She smiled, but he could tell it was forced.

"You're opposed to the idea?"

"No, I'm not. Everyone knows she's a Garrett, anyway, so it makes sense to make it official."

"You don't sound thrilled."

"I just think it will be strange, for me, when her name's different than mine."

"Yours could be changed, too," he suggested, "if you married me."

Okay, so it wasn't the most romantic proposal—it wasn't even a proposal, really—but she didn't even blink.

"I've been Kelly Cooper for too long to start answering to something different now."

"You could have given the idea some consideration before dismissing it out of hand," he grumbled.

"I got married once for the wrong reasons, Jacks. I'm not going to do it again."

"What if it wasn't for the wrong reasons?"

She still didn't blink, but she did seem to consider his question before responding this time. "Is that a hypothetical question?"

"For the moment." Because as sure as he was about his feelings for Kelly, he was too unsure of hers to put his heart on the line just yet.

"Then I would say that, hypothetically, I'm not opposed to the idea of marriage."

For now, that was good enough for Jack.

Sleepovers at a friend's house were one of the very best rites of childhood, so when Laurel invited Ava to spend Friday night at her house, Kelly didn't even consider refusing the request. She knew they would probably eat junk food, talk about boys, paint their toenails, eat more junk food and stay up too late, and that Ava would be overtired and cranky on Saturday, but Kelly didn't mind.

She knew Laurel and Laurel's parents and she had absolutely no reason at all to be apprehensive about the fact that her daughter was sleeping over at a friend's house. And she wasn't. Nor did she mind being alone in the house. It was the possibility that she might be alone in the house *with* Jackson that had her worried.

But when she got home from dropping Ava off at her friend's house, there was a message on the machine from Jackson, telling her that he wasn't going to be home until late because he was going to help Lukas fix his fence. Apparently his "genius dog" had somehow found a way—or at least a place—to get under it. Listening to his voice on the machine, Kelly told herself that she was relieved and not disappointed. She was glad the brothers were mending fences—figuratively as well as literally.

She would still make her seafood fettuccine Alfredo, but she would make it for one instead of two. And she would even have a glass of wine with her pasta. She'd bought a sauvignon blanc that she knew would complement the cream sauce and she wasn't going to deprive herself just because she was dining alone. After she'd finished eating and cleaned up the kitchen, she poured a second glass and took it up to the bath.

It was a rare event for her to have the house to herself, so she was going to indulge in a soak in the tub. She added bubbles and lit some candles and told herself she had everything she wanted. She didn't need a man to complete the picture.

But with her body feeling loose and warm from the bath and her mind pleasantly fuzzy from the wine, she couldn't deny there were times when she missed having a man around. Times when she missed Jacks. She pulled the plug to drain the tub and wished she could empty her mind of thoughts of her daughter's father so easily.

It didn't take Jack and Luke long to figure out where Einstein was going under the fence. As soon as his master let him into the yard, the puppy made a beeline for the back corner, where the ground dipped just slightly. And Einstein was little enough to be able to squeeze under the boards.

They secured a piece of two-by-four horizontally across the bottom of the other fence boards and, as an added precaution, shoved a big rock against the post.

"Well, that was an easier fix than I expected," Luke said.

"That doesn't mean you get to renege on the offer of pizza and beer," Jack warned.

"I'm not reneging," his brother assured him. "I just figured whatever Kelly's making is probably better than pizza."

Jack shrugged. "I already told her I wouldn't be there for dinner."

So Lukas ordered the pizza and popped open a couple of beers.

"What's going on with you and Kelly?" he asked when the pizza box was empty.

"Nothing," Jack said.

"Then why don't you want to go home?"

There was no point in denying that he didn't. "Because there's nothing going on."

Lukas nodded his understanding. "She's got you all tied up in knots, doesn't she?"

"You don't have to sound so damn pleased about it," he grumbled.

"But I am pleased. When I finally put two and two together and realized that you were the guy who got my best friend pregnant, I was furious—"

"Were you?" Jack casually rubbed a hand over his jaw. "I didn't notice."

His brother just shrugged, unapologetic. "I was furious with you because I was sure that you'd somehow taken advantage of Kelly," he continued. "But the more I've seen you with her, the more I've started to wonder if she wasn't the one who took advantage of you."

"Yeah, I tried to fight her off, but she overpowered me," he said dryly.

Luke chuckled. "Women might look all soft and feminine, but when it comes right down to it, they have the power because they make us weak."

"Aren't you in a philosophical mood tonight?"

"Am I wrong?"

Jack thought about it for a minute, shook his head. "No, you're not wrong."

"So what are you going to do about it?" his brother demanded.

"I'm going to marry her," he said simply.

Luke's jaw dropped open. "Well, hell, Jack, that isn't quite the answer I was expecting."

"I've been thinking about it for a while," he admitted.

"Do you love her?"

"It seems that I do."

"I hope you manage to sound a little more enthusiastic than that when you tell Kelly how you feel."

"It's hard to be enthusiastic about something so terrifying," Jack admitted.

"If it wasn't scary, it wouldn't be real."

"How would you know?"

"Because I've never been scared," Luke admitted.

He considered that while he finished his beer.

When he set down the empty bottle, his brother said, "Go home, Jack."

"That's the thanks I get for helping to fix your fence?"

"We nailed up one board," Luke reminded him. "Go home to your woman and you can thank me later."

Jack decided that was good advice.

Kelly toweled off and dressed in her favorite pajamas. They were soft flannel and covered in pictures of candy hearts, but they were her favorite because they'd been a Mother's Day gift from Ava last year. She had just settled on the couch with a DVD and a third glass of wine when she heard a key in the door.

"I thought you were helping Lukas tonight," she said when Jackson came in.

"I did. We finished." He settled on the other end of the sofa. "Where's Ava?"

She swallowed. "At Laurel's."

He nodded toward the bottle of wine on the table, and the half-filled glass beside it. "She's spending the night?"

She nodded. It was an easy assumption to make, because he knew she didn't drink if she was going to be driving. She also didn't indulge—at least not in more than one glass—around Jackson. She had enough trouble thinking straight when he was around without alcohol fogging her brain.

"Are you going to finish the bottle yourself or can I have a glass?"

"Help yourself," she said, wishing he would go away again. She didn't want to be alone with him, not when her preteen chaperone was away and her blood was already humming in her veins.

"What are you watching?"

"Casablanca," she told him.

He settled deeper into the sofa, but she felt his gaze on

her. "I've never actually seen the end of this movie," he admitted. "In fact, I don't think I've seen anything beyond the first half hour that we watched at that second-run theater the weekend I spent with you in Chicago."

Kelly reached for her glass and sipped her wine.

"You didn't think I even remembered what movie we'd gone to see, did you?" he challenged. "The movie that we walked out of because we wanted so desperately to be together that seeing the end of the movie didn't matter."

"Young lust," she said lightly.

"That's what I thought," he admitted. "What I hoped. That the desire I felt for you would be easily sated. But it wasn't. It didn't seem to matter how many times I had you that weekend, it wasn't enough."

"It was a long time ago."

"More than thirteen years—and in all that time, I never forgot how you felt in my arms. I never stopped wanting you."

She looked up at him, tears shimmering in her eyes. "You're not playing fair."

"All's fair in love and war," he reminded her.

She didn't know if this was love or war. She only knew that she loved him, that she'd never stopped loving him. She didn't really know how he felt about her. He'd told her that she was under his skin and in his heart, but he hadn't actually said that he loved her. But she knew he was physically attracted to her and, right now, with his body angled toward her and his mouth hovering mere inches above hers, that was enough.

She lifted her arms, linked them behind his head and brought his mouth down to hers. She kissed him, deeply, hungrily. Using her lips and her teeth and her tongue, she told him what she wanted, how much she wanted.

After several minutes, Jackson drew away, his breathing ragged. "How much of that wine have you drank?"

"Enough. But not too much." She nibbled on his bottom lip. "I know what I'm doing."

She wasn't sure she wouldn't have regrets in the morning, but right now, she knew she would regret it even more if she didn't give in—not just to the desire pulsing in her veins, but the feelings in her heart.

He lifted her into his arms and carried her the short distance to his bedroom. He set her gently on her feet beside the bed, but it wasn't until he started to unbutton her pajama top that she remembered what she was wearing.

"Obviously I didn't dress for seduction," she said.

"You're sexy no matter what you're wearing." He slipped the top off of her shoulders, then pushed her pants over her hips so they pooled at her feet. "And even sexier in nothing at all."

She wanted him in nothing at all, too, and quickly stripped away his clothes. He eased her down on top of the mattress, then stretched out beside her. She reached for him eagerly, ready for the hot and hungry demand of his mouth on hers, ready for the fast and frantic pass of his hands over her body, ready for the relentless and dizzying drive to the peak.

But Jackson apparently had different ideas, because when he kissed her this time, there was patience to temper the passion, tenderness layered over desire. He brushed her hair gently away from her face and feathered kisses over her cheeks, along her jaw, down her throat. The soft brush of his mouth against her skin made her burn; the tender stroke of strong male hands made her quiver.

"You're trembling," he noted.

"I'm a little nervous," she admitted.

"We have done this once or twice before."

They had, and yet— "Not like this."

He smiled as his fingertips skimmed over her, a tender caress. "No, not like this," he agreed. "I've never before made love with you knowing that I was in love with you." His mouth brushed over hers. "I do love you, Kelly."

She wanted to believe him. She desperately wanted to believe that this was real, that it could last forever. But she was afraid to hope, to want, to believe.

"Jacks—"

"I don't need you to say anything," he told her. "Not yet."

He covered her mouth again, so that words were impossible. Then he deepened the kiss, until her mind was spinning and her body was aching, and he took her hands in his, linked their fingers together.

And when he finally slipped inside of her, they were connected as intimately as any two people could be.

Chapter Fourteen

In the warmth of Jackson's embrace, Kelly had to admit that all her warnings to herself had been for naught. She was in love with him. Undeniably and irrevocably. Just because she hadn't said the words out loud didn't mean it wasn't true.

The first love that she'd experienced as a sixteen-year-old had been little more than a girl's innocent infatuation. She'd been a woman when they'd met again, with a woman's heart and a woman's desires. Her feelings for him had been intense and overwhelming, but without much of a foundation. She'd loved the man she wanted him to be, then hated him when he'd broken her heart, but she'd never really known him.

Since coming back to Pinehurst, she'd realized how misconceived her own emotions had been. She'd accepted that he wasn't a hero any more than he was a villain. He was simply a man. He had strengths and weaknesses, virtues and faults. He was a dedicated attorney, a caring father, a loyal friend, an incredible lover. He could be arrogant and obstinate, but he was undeniably the man she loved.

"Okay." He stroked a hand lazily down her spine. "You can say it now."

She propped her chin up on his chest. "What was it that I'm supposed to say?"

"That you love me."

Oh, yeah, he was arrogant. And sexy. And she was completely head over heels. "I love you, Jackson."

She shifted so that she could press her mouth to his, and the delicious friction of her naked skin against his set off sparks all over her body.

His arms banded around her, holding her tight against him as he deepened the kiss. They'd just finished making love, but sprawled on top of him as she was, she could tell that his body was fired up again, too.

"Energetic." She murmured the word against his lips.

He drew back. "What?"

"I was making a mental list of your virtues and faults," she admitted. "And I realized that I should add 'energetic.'"

"What faults?" he demanded, sounding so indignant she couldn't help but laugh.

"Your super-size ego would be at the top of the list."

With his hands on her hips, Jack shifted her so that her soft feminine center was pressed against the hard length of his erection. "You were saying something about a super-size—"

"Ego!"

He just grinned and continued to rub against her, a slow, sensual caress. He heard the catch in her breath, saw the escalation of desire in her eyes.

"Energetic and insatiable," she said.

"It's your fault," he told her. "No one has ever made me want the way you do."

She smiled as she rose up, gloriously naked and stunningly beautiful. Her long dark hair tumbled over her shoulders, and her eyes—those gorgeous golden eyes—burned with fire when she positioned herself over him. Her gaze stayed locked on his as she angled her hips and took him inside of her.

His fingers tightened on her flesh as he fought for control. She was so hot and wet and tight, and his body was desperate to mate with hers. He had to battle against the instinctive urge to take, to claim, to possess, and focused on caressing, teasing, pleasuring. He let his hands skim over her torso, from her hips to her breasts. His thumbs circled her nipples, moving slowly but inexorably closer to the tight peaks. Her breath quickened, her body tensed. She was close to the edge, teetering on the precipice.

He'd been with a lot of women, but only with Kelly had the reality of making love outdistanced the fantasy. And he knew the reason had as much to do with the connection between their hearts as the joining of their bodies.

She was the one who had left Pinehurst, but it wasn't until she came back that he truly found where he belonged, because it was with her. She loved him, too. It didn't bother him that she hadn't volunteered the words, because he didn't doubt her feelings any longer. He could see her love for him in her eyes. He could taste it on her lips. He could feel it in the warmth of the body that embraced his.

As they moved together now, he knew that it was more than the giving and taking of pleasure—it was sharing and loving. And together, they finally tumbled over the edge.

Kelly squinted at the glowing numbers on the clock and resigned herself to getting out of bed…soon. She'd told Claire that she would pick up Ava around noon, and it was already ten o'clock. She couldn't remember the last time she'd slept so late. On the other hand, she couldn't remember the last time she'd spent most of the night making love. And while she was physically exhausted, she was also incredibly happy.

When 10:14 became 10:15, she eased toward the edge of the mattress—then let out a yelp when Jack's arm snaked around her waist and hauled her back against him.

"Where do you think you're going?" he demanded, his voice still rough with sleep.

"To pick up our daughter."

"But it's not even morning yet," he protested. "It can't be morning—we haven't slept."

"It's not only morning, it's late, and I need a shower."

She wriggled out of his hold, and Jack, with a groan of protest, shifted to sit up.

He looked so cute and grumpy in her bed, she couldn't resist him. She brushed a soft kiss on his lips. "Go back to sleep."

He scrubbed his hands over his face. "If I don't get up, I'll miss out on shower sex."

"I don't have time to go another round with you right now," she told him, but she couldn't deny that the outrageously blunt statement made her tingle.

"If you've got time to shower, you've got time for shower sex. It's basic multitasking."

"Well, I do like to multitask."

He grinned and dragged her into the adjoining bath. "I know."

"We should probably decide what we're going to tell Ava about...this development," Kelly said as she fastened the buttons on her blouse.

Jacks, already dressed, lounged on her bed watching her. "I have no doubt that she will be completely onboard."

"You don't think it will be a little weird for her...her mother and her father...dating."

His lips curved. "Is that what we're doing?"

She wiggled into a pair of jeans. "I'm *not* going to tell her that we're having sex."

"I agree that the 'dating' thing might be weird," he admitted. "Maybe it would be easier for Ava if we just got married."

The brush she'd picked up to drag through her still-damp hair slipped from her fingers, and she slowly drew in a deep breath as she bent to retrieve it. "Is that another hypothetical, Jackson?"

"No." The fingers of one hand circled her wrist, drawing her toward him, as his other hand dipped into the pocket of his jeans. "It's a proposal."

Her heart lodged in her throat when she recognized the Diamond Jubilee logo on the top of the box.

Once, a very long time ago, Kelly had let herself dream about marrying Jackson. Then he had married someone else, and she'd moved on with her life. She'd married and divorced, and she'd never forgotten him. Even when she'd decided to move back to Pinehurst, she hadn't let herself think that she could have any kind of a future with Jackson. She hadn't, until recently, even realized that it was what she wanted.

But now, she knew that there was nothing she wanted more. To marry the man that she loved, the father of her child, to be a family—it was everything.

He flipped open the lid and her heart jolted again.

"It's stunning."

"Ava helped me pick it out," he told her.

"You took Ava shopping for an engagement ring?"

"I wanted a second opinion," he said reasonably. "And I couldn't think of anyone whose opinion would matter more to either of us than our daughter's."

"You were right," she murmured. "And she has impeccable taste."

"You like it?"

She didn't have any words to tell him what the ring meant to her—not because of its shape or size, but because it proved that he loved her enough to make a commitment to her. So she kissed him. Long and slow and deep.

It wasn't until Jack started unfastening her blouse and she wondered why she'd even bothered to put clothes on that she suddenly remembered the reason.

She pulled away from him abruptly. "We have to get Ava."

Jack sighed with obvious reluctance. "Do you really think the Lamontagnes would mind if we were just a little bit late?"

"As much as I'm sure Ava had a fabulous time, I think she's probably anxious to get home."

But as it happened, Laurel's mom called Kelly's cell while they were en route and asked if Ava could stay for a little bit longer. Apparently the girls had stayed up late (as Kelly had expected) and slept late (which she had not anticipated), so their plans to go bowling in the morning had been pushed back—if that was okay.

Of course Kelly said that it was. But since they were already out of the house, Jackson decided to stop by his condo to pick up some legal texts that he wanted to review for an upcoming trial.

The first thing Kelly noticed when she stepped through the door was the shoes. There was no way she could have missed them. The sling-backs with skyscraper heels were like a bloodred stain in the middle of his ivory carpet.

Before her brain could even wrap around the implications, a throaty feminine purr came from down the hall. From his bedroom. "Jackson?"

Jack didn't know how to interpret Kelly's shocked expression. Was it shocked disbelief? Or shocked disappointment? He could only imagine what she was thinking. He knew it hadn't been easy for her to overlook his wild past, to believe that he'd changed. And now that past had reared its ugly head and was threatening to destroy his only chance at happiness.

"Kelly—" He heard the desperate plea in his own voice. "I swear to you, this is not what you're thinking."

The shock that had been so evident only a minute before had been carefully masked so that her face was expressionless now. And her voice, when she spoke, was calm. "I'm thinking there's a woman in your bed."

He shook his head, because he didn't want it to be true. "If there is, she wasn't invited," he promised.

Kelly didn't respond, but she made her way down the hall, following the trail of discarded undergarments. She picked up stockings, a tiny wisp that might have been panties, a matching bra, a dress. He followed in her path, feeling helpless and desperate and—when he saw Norah in his bed—absolutely furious.

He knew it looked bad. Hell, he couldn't imagine any scene that might look worse. And it was immediately apparent to him that this was a scene carefully staged by Norah for maximum effect.

He didn't think her plan had been for anything more complicated than seduction. She couldn't have planned to sabotage his relationship with Kelly because she had no way of knowing that he would bring her to his condo.

When Norah saw Kelly standing in the doorway, the widening of her eyes confirmed her surprise. She'd obviously expected him to be alone. But she recovered quickly, and the slow, satisfied smile that curved her lips proved that she didn't give a damn who got hurt as long as she got what she wanted.

He wasn't gullible enough to believe that she really wanted him. Maybe she'd considered that they would have some fun together and be lovers for a while, and if he'd gone along with her plan, that likely would have been the end of it. But Jack had resisted her advances, and she apparently wasn't going to tolerate any man resisting her.

But Norah's motives and machinations were the least of his concerns right now. All that mattered to him was Kelly. He'd been the happiest man in the world when she agreed to marry him. Now, he felt as if his happiness was slipping through his fingers, like grains of sand in an hourglass.

Dammit, she'd said that she loved him. He would have thought that love would be accompanied by at least a little bit of faith, but he could read nothing in her eyes. He held her gaze, silently begging her to trust him, to believe him, to love him enough. He wanted to plead with her; he was willing to beg. But in that moment he realized that if she didn't trust him enough to know that he loved her too much to even think about another woman when he was with her, then they didn't have any kind of foundation to build a future together.

Kelly didn't say anything to him, but she carried the pile of clothing she'd collected to the bed and dumped it on top of the covers. "Get dressed and get out."

One of Norah's perfectly arched brows lifted. "Who the hell are you?"

"I'm Jackson's lover, the mother of his child, and the woman he's going to marry. And you have three seconds to get your clothes on and get out of here before I toss you into the hall buck naked."

Something in her tone must have convinced Norah that she meant what she said, because she gathered up the pile of clothes and retreated to the bathroom.

"Kelly—"

She shook her head. "I don't want to talk about this until she's gone."

"Okay," he agreed.

He didn't think it took Norah much more than the allotted three seconds to get dressed, but it seemed like forever. Three interminable seconds in which his life hung in the balance.

When she came out of the bathroom, she looked chastened but unrepentant, and she didn't look at him but at Kelly. "I figured the 'Jack-pot' was worth a gamble." She smiled at her own joke, shrugged.

"Was it worth going to jail?" Jack wanted to know. "Because right now, I'm tempted to call the cops to have you booked for breaking and entering."

She tossed her hair over her shoulder. "It's not breaking and entering when you have a key."

"And where in hell did you get a key?"

The fury in his voice must have registered, because she quickly explained. "I have a key to Marcy's apartment, and I knew that she had a key to yours. I was at her place to return a jacket I borrowed when I saw your car pull into the parking lot, and I thought…I guess I thought wrong."

"Where's the key now?" he asked.

She handed it over and walked out the door.

Kelly turned and followed the other woman's path to the living room. She stood at the window, her arms folded across her chest, her expression still blank.

"Talk to me, please," Jack said to her. "Tell me what you're thinking."

"My head is spinning, and the image of that woman naked in your bed isn't likely to fade anytime soon."

Before he could consider a response to that, she switched mental gears and asked, "Who's Marcy and why did she have a key?"

"Marcy is my neighbor across the hall. She's a real estate agent but she works mostly from home. A couple of months ago, her fax machine broke and she asked if she could borrow mine. She was in and out a lot to use the machine, so I gave her a key in case she needed access to it when I wasn't home. She got her machine fixed, but I never thought to get the key back."

"Why would she give the key to Miss Scarlet?"

"She wouldn't have," he answered without hesitation. "Marcy and Norah might be friends, but Marcy would never cross that line."

"But Norah would take it, because she knows how to get what she wants."

He nodded, impressed by the accuracy of her assessment.

"I don't know how I feel about the fact that women always seem to be throwing themselves at you," she admitted to him now.

"I think you should take into consideration the fact that I'm not catching any of them. That I don't want anyone but you."

"I'm trying to."

"You do know that she set this whole scene?"

She nodded, and the tightness around his chest finally eased.

"No doubts?"

"I never would have agreed to marry you if I didn't love you *and* trust you," she told him. "Absolutely and completely."

It was a testament of trust, a leap of faith, and exactly what he needed to hear. He reached for her now, sliding his arms around her waist and drawing her close.

"You did tell Norah that you're the woman I'm going to marry," he recalled. "But you never actually said yes."

And he'd been so distracted by her kiss, he hadn't thought about it at the time. It was only as they were leaving her place that he saw the box on the bed and he realized she hadn't given him a chance to put the ring on her finger. He'd grabbed it and shoved it in his pocket, but he took it out now and opened the lid.

"You never actually asked the question," she countered.

"Kelly Cooper, will you—"

"Yes."

His brows lifted. "Impatient," he said, even as he slid the ring on her finger.

"Excuse me?"

"If we're cataloguing faults, that's one of yours."

"I waited more than thirteen years for this ring," she told him. "I'd say that demonstrates an incredible amount of patience."

"Okay, maybe not impatient."

He lifted her hand and kissed the knuckle of her third finger, just above the ring he'd placed there. Then he kissed her—sealing the promise they'd just made to one another.

When he finally eased his lips from hers, Kelly said, "Go find whatever books you need so we can go and get our daughter."

He sighed. "Bossy."

She laughed.

"I should probably warn you," Jack said, as he gathered the books together. "When Ava and I were shopping for rings, she had some very definite opinions—and some very specific expectations."

"About what?" she asked warily.

"Expanding our family."

Her gaze narrowed. "Did you promise her a puppy?"

"Actually, I think she's got her eye on Puss and Boots now," he said. "But she wants a little brother or sister even more."

Her heart bumped against her ribs.

As an only child herself, she'd envied the Garrett brothers the camaraderie and companionship they shared. And as much as Ava had always dreamed of having a brother or a sister, Kelly had wanted a sibling for her just as much. But she'd given up hope that it would ever happen, and now Jack was dangling the possibility in front of her—and it was even more dazzling than the diamond on her finger.

"I could go along with that plan," she said cautiously. "If you were in agreement."

"I can't think of anything that would make me happier," he said, with such sincerity it brought tears to her eyes. "And I promise you, here and now, if we do have another baby, I will be there every step of the way. From now until forever."

"I'll hold you to that," she warned him.

"I'm counting on it."

"Can I ask you a legal question?"

"Sure."

"Can a lawyer fire a client?"

"One step ahead of you on that," he promised.

Then he took her hand and they walked out of his condo, side by side, toward their future together.

* * * * *

Don't miss Lukas Garrett's story,
A VERY SPECIAL DELIVERY
the third installment in Brenda Harlen's new
Special Edition miniseries,
THOSE ENGAGING GARRETTS!
On sale September 2013, wherever
Harlequin books are sold.

REQUEST YOUR FREE BOOKS!

2 FREE NOVELS PLUS 2 FREE GIFTS!

⟨H⟩HARLEQUIN®

SPECIAL EDITION

Life, Love & Family

YES! Please send me 2 FREE Harlequin® Special Edition novels and my 2 FREE gifts (gifts are worth about $10). After receiving them, if I don't wish to receive any more books, I can return the shipping statement marked "cancel." If I don't cancel, I will receive 6 brand-new novels every month and be billed just $4.74 per book in the U.S. or $5.24 per book in Canada. That's a savings of at least 14% off the cover price! It's quite a bargain! Shipping and handling is just 50¢ per book in the U.S. and 75¢ per book in Canada.* I understand that accepting the 2 free books and gifts places me under no obligation to buy anything. I can always return a shipment and cancel at any time. Even if I never buy another book, the two free books and gifts are mine to keep forever.

235/335 HDN F45Y

Name	(PLEASE PRINT)	
Address		Apt. #
City	State/Prov.	Zip/Postal Code

Signature (if under 18, a parent or guardian must sign)

Mail to the **Harlequin® Reader Service:**
IN U.S.A.: P.O. Box 1867, Buffalo, NY 14240-1867
IN CANADA: P.O. Box 609, Fort Erie, Ontario L2A 5X3

Want to try two free books from another line?
Call 1-800-873-8635 or visit www.ReaderService.com.

* Terms and prices subject to change without notice. Prices do not include applicable taxes. Sales tax applicable in N.Y. Canadian residents will be charged applicable taxes. Offer not valid in Quebec. This offer is limited to one order per household. Not valid for current subscribers to Harlequin Special Edition books. All orders subject to credit approval. Credit or debit balances in a customer's account(s) may be offset by any other outstanding balance owed by or to the customer. Please allow 4 to 6 weeks for delivery. Offer available while quantities last.

Your Privacy—The Harlequin® Reader Service is committed to protecting your privacy. Our Privacy Policy is available online at www.ReaderService.com or upon request from the Harlequin Reader Service.

We make a portion of our mailing list available to reputable third parties that offer products we believe may interest you. If you prefer that we not exchange your name with third parties, or if you wish to clarify or modify your communication preferences, please visit us at www.ReaderService.com/consumerchoice or write to us at Harlequin Reader Service Preference Service, P.O. Box 9062, Buffalo, NY 14269. Include your complete name and address.

HSE13R

*When city girl Lissa Roarke comes to
Rust Creek Falls to assist with the cleanup efforts after
the Great Montana Flood, she butts heads with
Sheriff Gage Christensen. He doesn't trust outsiders,
and seems bent on making Lissa's life miserable.
Little does he know that she's the cure for what ails him....*

***

"I'm so excited I can't stand it," she admitted. "We can finally
start getting something done."

Her enthusiasm burrowed inside him. He smiled. "Yeah,
that's good. And we all appreciate it."

"Thanks," she said. "I'm going to make an early night of it,
so I'll be ready to greet the volunteers tomorrow. Thank you
for getting me some wheels."

"My pleasure," Gage said. "But no—"

"Driving in the snow," she finished for him. "That ditch
was no fun for me, either."

"It's dark. You want me to walk you back to the rooming
house?" He offered because he wanted to extend his time with
her.

"I think I'll be okay," she said. "Rust Creek isn't the most crime-
ridden place in the world. But thank you for your chivalry."

Gage gave a rough chuckle. "No one's ever accused me of
being chivalrous."

"Well, maybe they haven't been watching closely enough."

Gage felt his gut take a hard dip at her statement. He knew

that Lissa was struggling with her visit to Rust Creek and he hadn't made it as easy for her as he should have. There was some kind of electricity or something between them that he couldn't quite name. Just looking at her did something to him.

"I'll take that as a compliment. Call me if you need me," he said.

"Thank you," she said. "Good night."

"Good night," he said, and wished she was going home with him to his temporary trailer to keep him warm. Crazy, he told himself. All wrong. She was Manhattan. He was Montana. Big difference. The twain would never meet. Right?

***

We hope you enjoyed this sneak peek from
USA TODAY bestselling author Leanne Banks's new
Harlequin Special Edition book,
THE MAVERICK & THE MANHATTANITE,
the next installment in
MONTANA MAVERICKS: RUST CREEK COWBOYS,
the brand-new six-book continuity launched in July 2013!

HSEEXP0813

SADDLE UP AND READ 'EM!

Looking for another great Western read? Check out these September reads from HOME & FAMILY category!

CALLAHAN COWBOY TRIPLETS by Tina Leonard
Callahan Cowboys
Harlequin American Romance

HAVING THE COWBOY'S BABY by Trish Milburn
Blue Falls, Texas
Harlequin American Romance

HOME TO WYOMING by Rebecca Winters
Daddy Dude Ranch
Harlequin American Romance

Look for these great Western reads and more available wherever books are sold or visit
www.Harlequin.com/Westerns

Be sure to check out the first book in this year's
FAMILY RENEWAL miniseries
by bestselling author Sheri WhiteFeather.

During high school, Ryan Nash dated Victoria Allen.
When Victoria got pregnant, they turned to adoption.
However, when Ryan failed to show up for their
daughter's birth, Victoria never spoke to him again.
Fast-forward eighteen years later and both Victoria
and her daughter, Kaley, have set out on a search for
each other. A slow and steady bond builds between
them, but when Kaley wants to meet her birth
father, will this family find their happily-ever-after?

*Look for LOST AND FOUND FATHER next month
from Harlequin® Special Edition® wherever books
and ebooks are sold!*

HSE65766

HARLEQUIN®

SPECIAL EDITION

Life, Love and Family

Be sure to check out the first book in this year's
THE CHERRY SISTERS trilogy
by reader-favorite author Lilian Darcy.

After spending a year abroad as a college exchange
student, Daisy Cherry returned for the wedding of
her sister Lee to Tucker Reid—completely unaware of
his instant attraction to her. He'd already been having
doubts over his wedding, so this was the catalyst for
calling it off. Ten years later the Cherry sisters have all
moved back to the upmarket Adirondack hotel resort
their parents ran before they retired, and with Tucker
running a successful business in town, sparks and
complications are sure to arise!

Look for
THE ONE WHO CHANGED EVERYTHING
*next month from Harlequin® Special Edition®
wherever books and ebooks are sold!*

www.Harlequin.com

HSE65764

Love the Harlequin book you just read?

Your opinion matters.

Review this book on your favorite book site, review site, blog or your own social media properties and share your opinion with other readers!